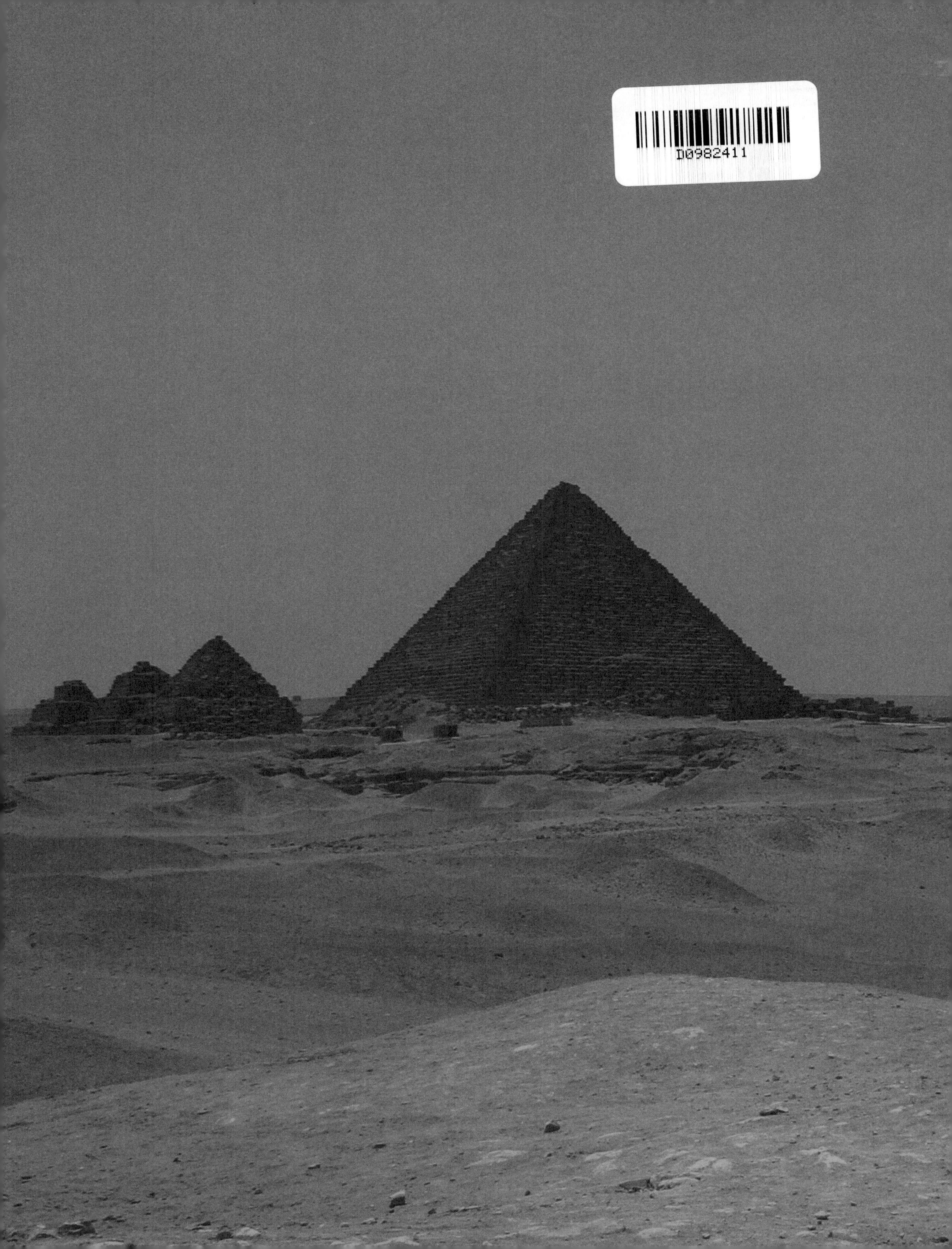

LONG LIVE ENTROPY!

Ty

& S

Authors: Barbora Klárová
Tomáš Končinský

po
kim

Illustrations: Daniel Špaček
Design: Petr Štěpán

1: W

i

respo

Fig 1

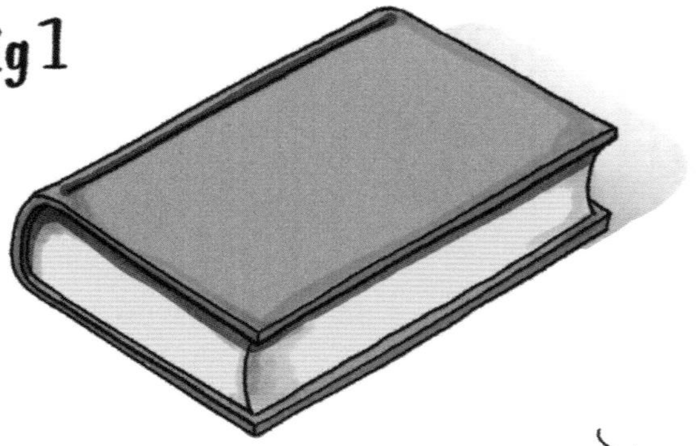

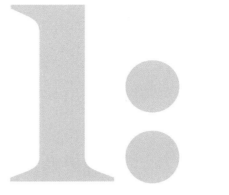

Fig 2

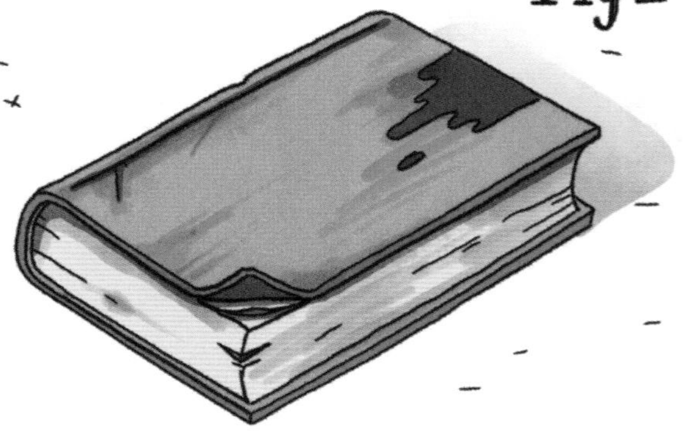

Fig 3

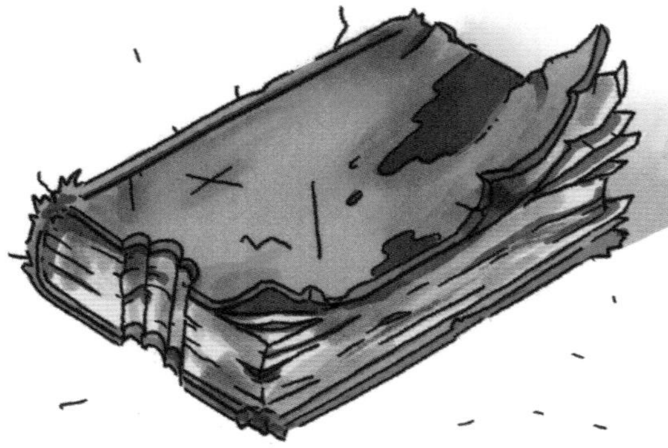

/ho
s
nsible

Fig 4

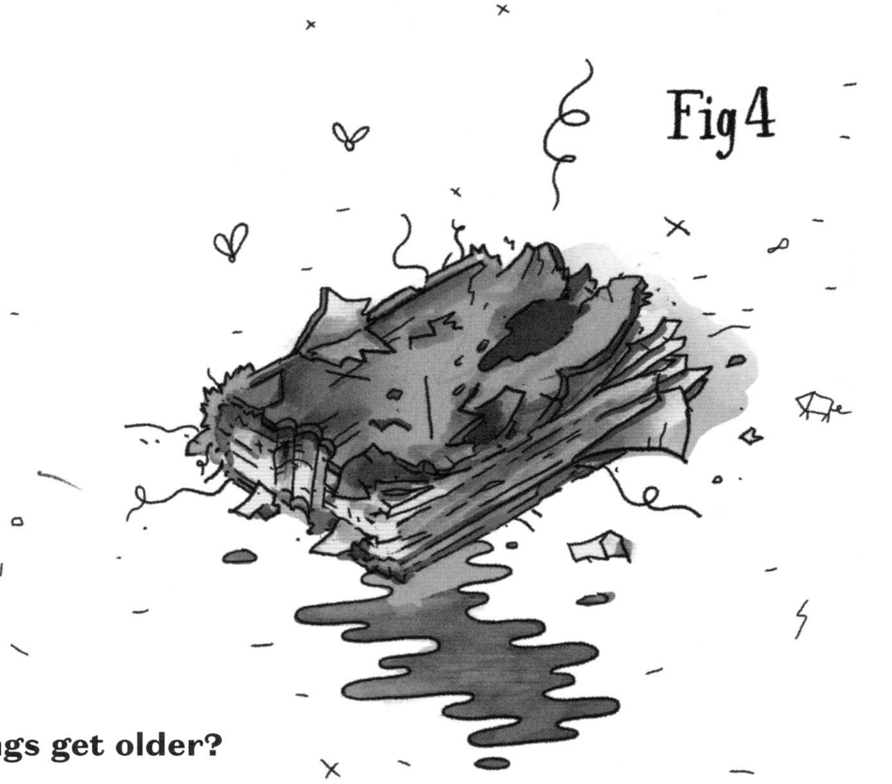

Have you noticed how things get older?

Of course you have. Who wouldn't notice such things? A toy that was brand-new is suddenly all scratched and falling apart. Your favorite T-shirt promptly has a hole in it, and the fun picture on it is fading out. That banana you forgot all about in your backpack a week ago – um, no, I'd better not write about that, some of you humans can get a bit squeamish about food...

Quite simply, everything ages. This book, too, will age and age until one day it falls apart. It seems like you turn your back, stop paying attention for just a second, and what was shiny and new a moment ago suddenly gets old. Who's responsible?

Well, I am!!!

Not me alone, of course. There are a few of us. Actually, quite a lot. In fact...there are so many of us it might make your skin crawl. Who are we, and what do we do exactly? I thought you'd never ask. Follow me and pay attention. The way we dispense of things is truly indispensable!

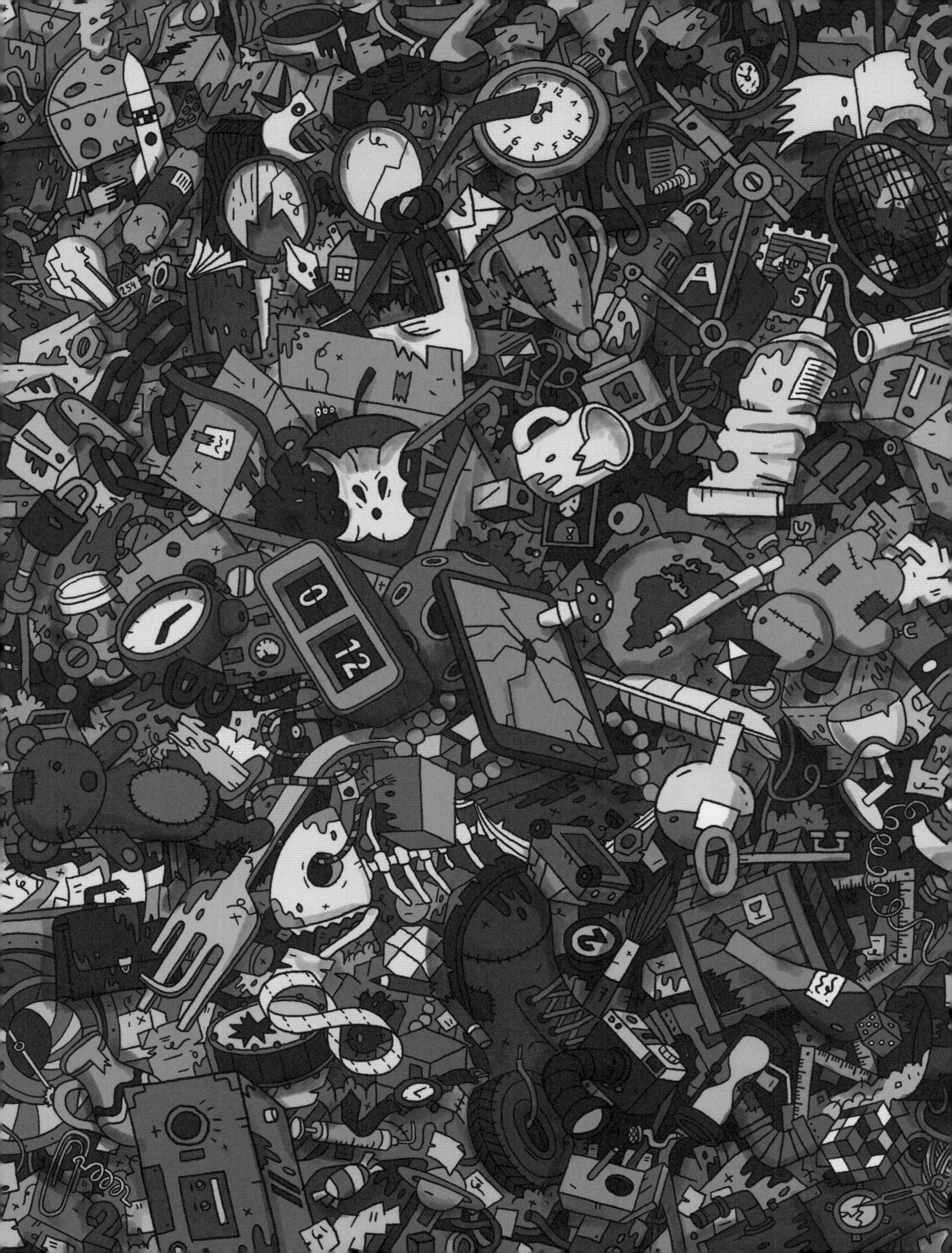

254
A
5
0
12

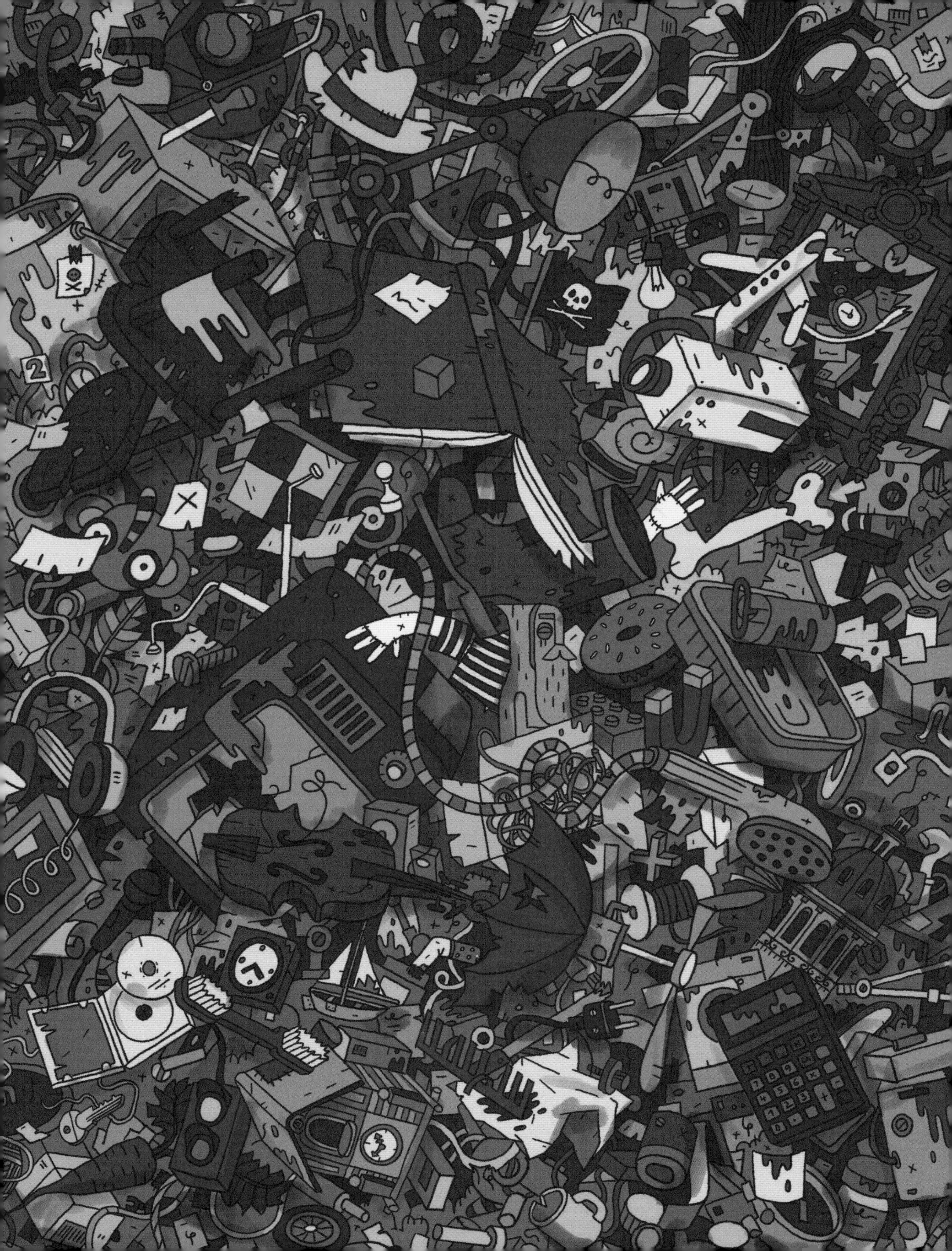

2: My

Ty

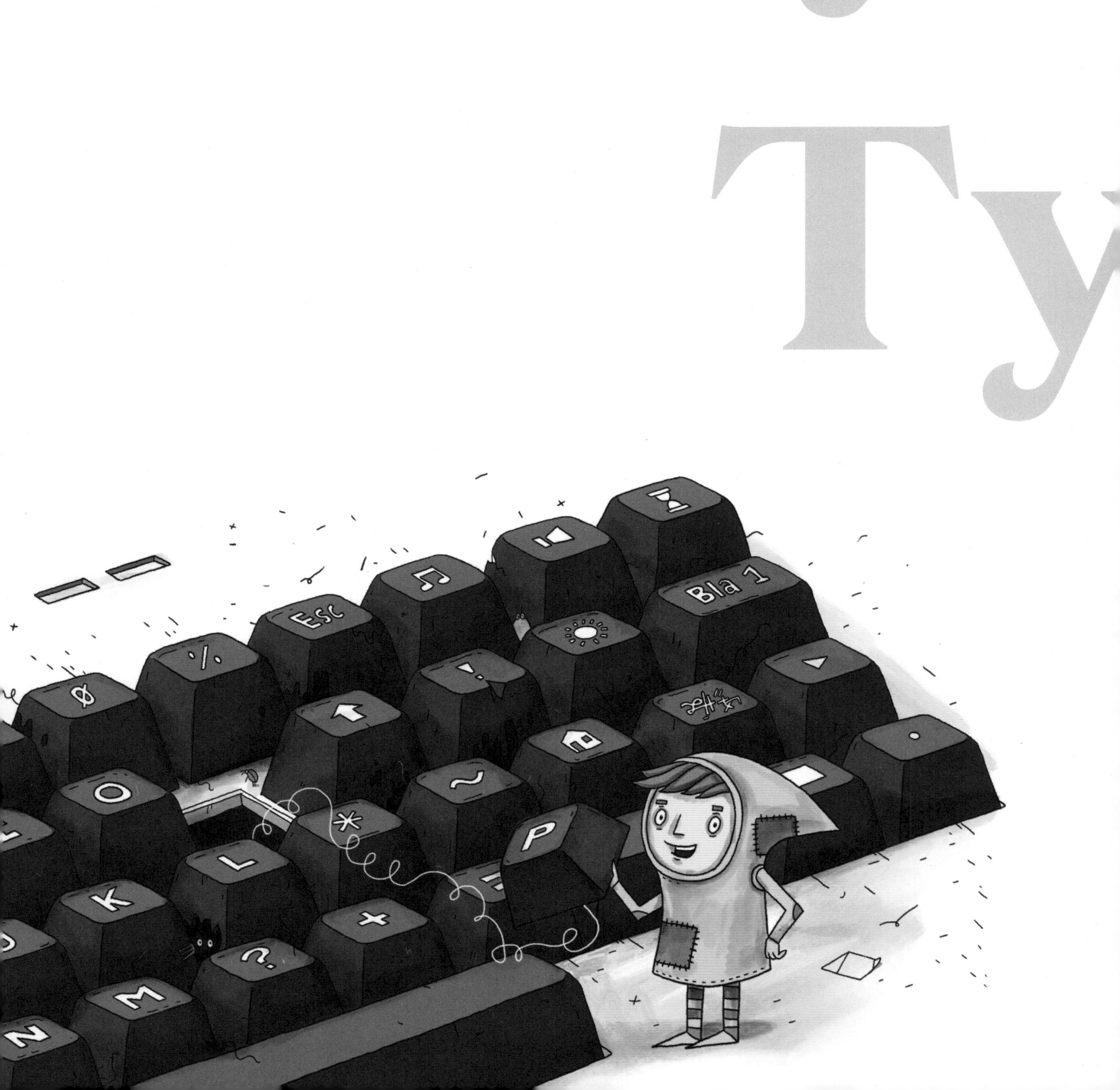

Bla 1
Esc
%
O
L
P
K
M
N

name's

po

Let me introduce myself.
My name's Typo.

I could write my name as Tpyo. Or Pyto. Maybe even Ptyo. Those are difficult to read and even more difficult to pronounce, but they're ever so funny! Why not try the same thing with your own name? You'll be amazed by how many forms it can take, unless your name is Ed or Eve or something. Typos are terrific fun!

Anyway, back to me. I'm an entropic elf. You're maybe thinking that an entropic elf has something to do with palms & coconuts. But our name relates to entropy, which basically means mess-making. Professor Block (more about him later) explains entropy in a very complicated way. But here's my simple analogy: Entropy is when you're playing Memory and you can't find any pairs; not only that, the cards keep getting lost. These problems are actually in the rules of Entromemory, and I should know because when we had an Entromemory tournament at our school last year, I triumphed. I'm a whiz at losing cards! Put simply, entropy is the confusion and disorder you see all around you, which we entropic elves bring about.

I'm still only in the third grade at PSAT – the Primary School for Aging Things. I may be young, but I'm a great help to my dad in the library. He takes me there once a week so I get some on the job experience. I look forward to finishing school and being able to do work of my own without supervision. The internet and programming attract me far more than libraries, though. Dad's not happy about this: he's worked with books all his life, and he doesn't understand the first thing about computers. More than anything, he'd like me to spring a typo on some successful writer because, if I did, my work would reach readers all over the world. I understand that it's a big deal to have a typo in some terribly famous book, but I think it's just as cool to have one in a program used by ten million people. But Dad won't hear of this, so I keep going with him to the library once a week, where I'm responsible for typos and other mess-ups in books, newspapers and magazines. How do I work? Don't be shy! I thought you'd never ask.

For instance, if a newspaper headline is supposed to say:

PRESIDENT TACKLES TEACHER

I get in there and make it into:

PRESIDENT TICKLES TEACHER

If the following is written in a book:

THE DRAGON-SLAYER
WON HALF A KINGDOM.

I make a little correction so that it reads:

THE DRAGON-SLAYER WON
A CALF KINGDOM.

The kind of word I like best of all is:

WILLIMOTESWICK

Just imagine all the things I could do with that!
Do you know any words that complicated? If you
do, please write them down on the notepad here.
I collect them, you see. Thanks a lot!

My dad says that I "just fool around" while he
does all the important, serious work. But I think
there's a good future in typos. Still, no doubt
that, as Head of the Department for Book Aging,
Dad has to work like a god. Sorry! like a dog.
Let me tell you something about that next...

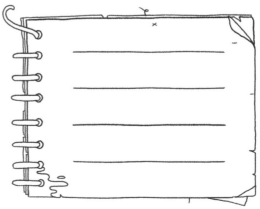

3: Depa
for I
Ag

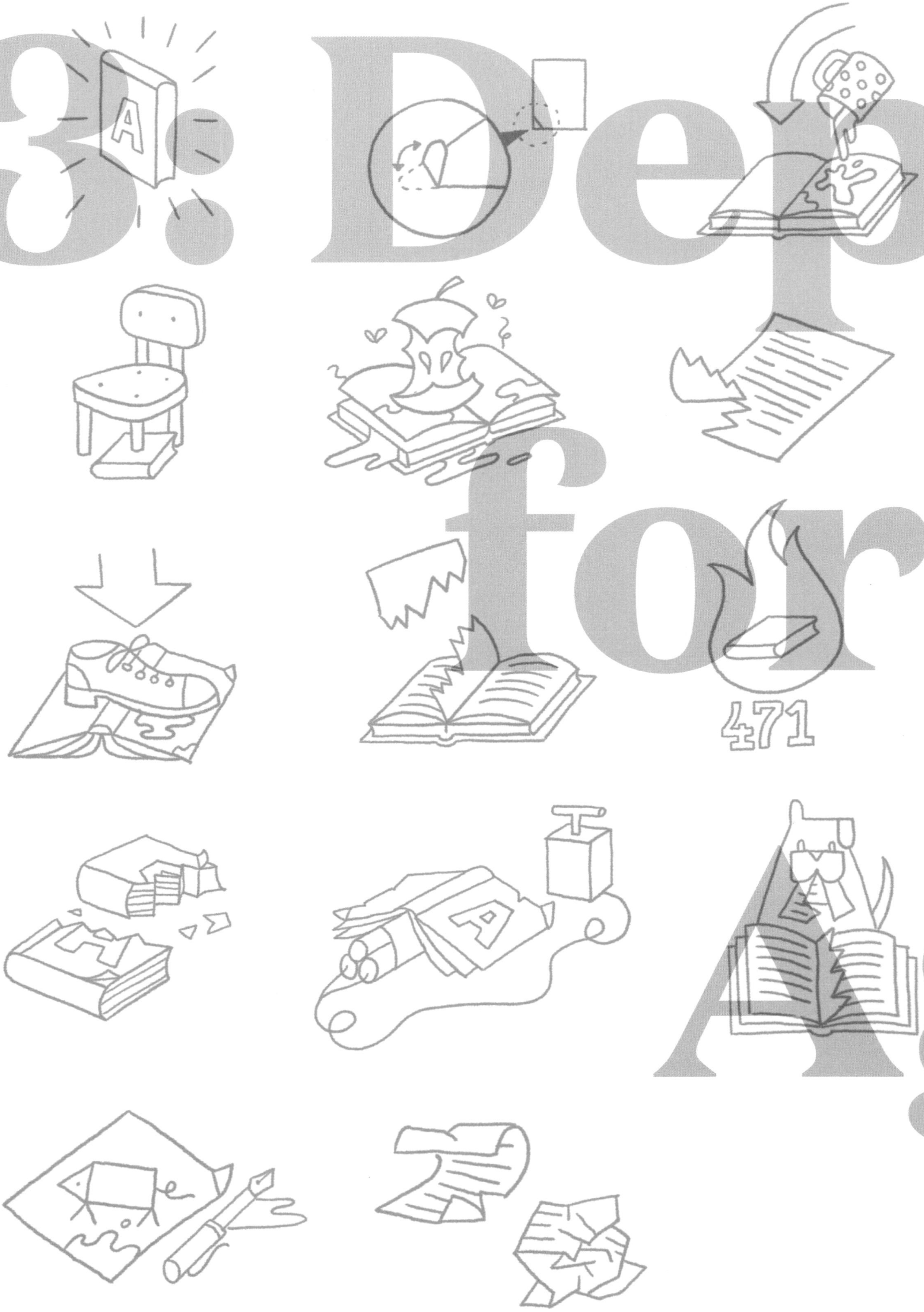
471

rtment

Book

ing

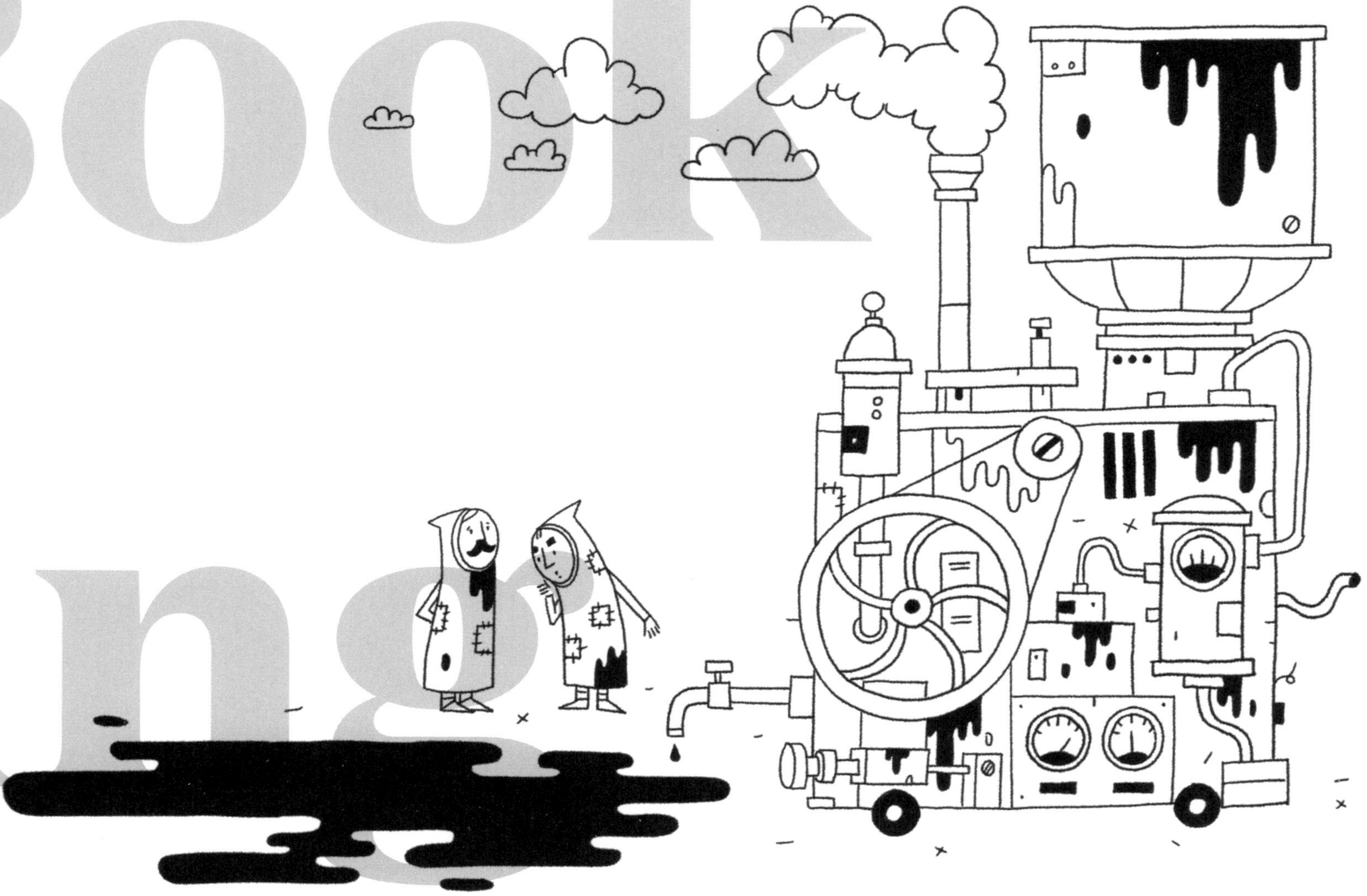

TWO-STROKE STEAM-POWERED CHOCO-SPLOTCHER

THIS SMEARING MECHANISM, INVENTED BY BRICKUS SWEET, REMAINS IN FREQUENT USAGE TODAY. OWING TO THE RELATIVELY HIGH HEAT LOSS DURING OPERATION, THE CHOCOLATE MELTS QUICKLY, MAKING IT EASIER TO DAB ON. A DRAWBACK IS ITS RELATIVELY GREAT WEIGHT, NECESSITATING THE USE OF 2–4 DRAFT SILVERFISH TO TOW IT.

TOMATO STAMP

THIS INNOCUOUS LITTLE CONTRIVANCE BY AMERICAN INVENTOR E. A. T. KETCHUP HAS TRULY REVOLUTIONIZED OUR ABILITY TO RENDER A TOMATO SPLAT.

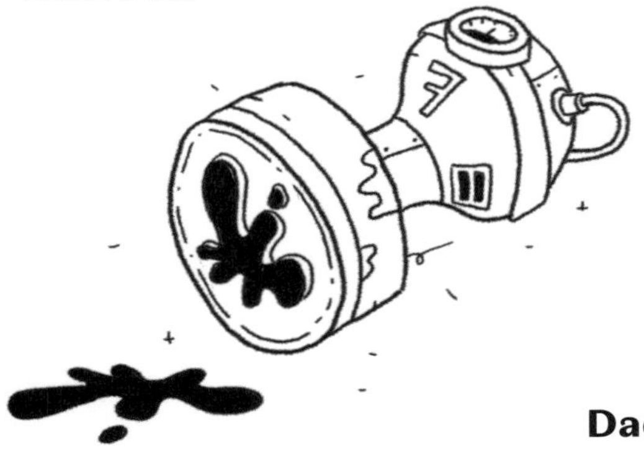

Has it ever happened that you've been unable to find your favorite book on the shelf at home? Search as you might, apparently it has disappeared into thin air. But don't worry, it hasn't really. OK, it has – but only for a short trip to my dad's department. Next time you go to that shelf, the book is sure to be on it. But it will look a bit older than you remember it.

Dad and his colleagues know lots of really great ways to make a brand new book look as a proper book should – with torn pages, dog-eared corners, smudges and so on; you know the sort of thing I mean from your own bookcase. Painters work day and night to make the ordinary white paper in a new book look lovely and dingy, either yellow or grey. They're helped in this by the corner-turners, hole-punchers and tearers, and sometimes too by the dunkers and letter-dissolvers. The snack team, who have their own division, make sure that a seemingly random page has nice traces of food pressed into it. I just love their tomato stamps, their oil and grease atomizers, and most of all their choco-splotcher. It's up to my dad to inspect and manage everything. I wouldn't want his job, I can tell you – it's really hard work!

My mom works in the Department for Book Aging too. She's in charge of the Fragrances Division. She works in a huge laboratory filled with vials, retorts and test tubes filled with dust, wet rot and all kinds of glorious mold. She's a wizard at mixing these together! Have you ever noticed that every book has a slightly different smell? If not, pull a few books from your bookcase. Have a sniff ... Now do you know what I mean? All this is my mom's work.

Although Mom is good to me, she's forever
telling me where and how I should be making
myself dirty, and what I need to tear or crumple.
Sometimes this gets on my nerves. If I come
home without at least a few drips of ice cream
on my pants, I'm in trouble. Also, I have to keep
my room in a mess – heaven help me if I put
my toys away in a drawer! Never try to tidy up
in front of my mom – not if you value your life!

Now that I've explained what we're all about, at last
it's time for me to tell you about the great adventure
me and my best friend Skim had not long ago. It took
us all the way to the great Cog of Time, which manages
and controls the aging of absolutely everything in
the world. Have you ever heard of it? It's the stuff
of legend for entropic elves, though no one has ever
actually seen it. At least, they hadn't. Until I did...
But let me start by telling you about Skim.

ARRANGEMENT OF A CHILD'S BEDROOM:
ATOM BOMB OPTION

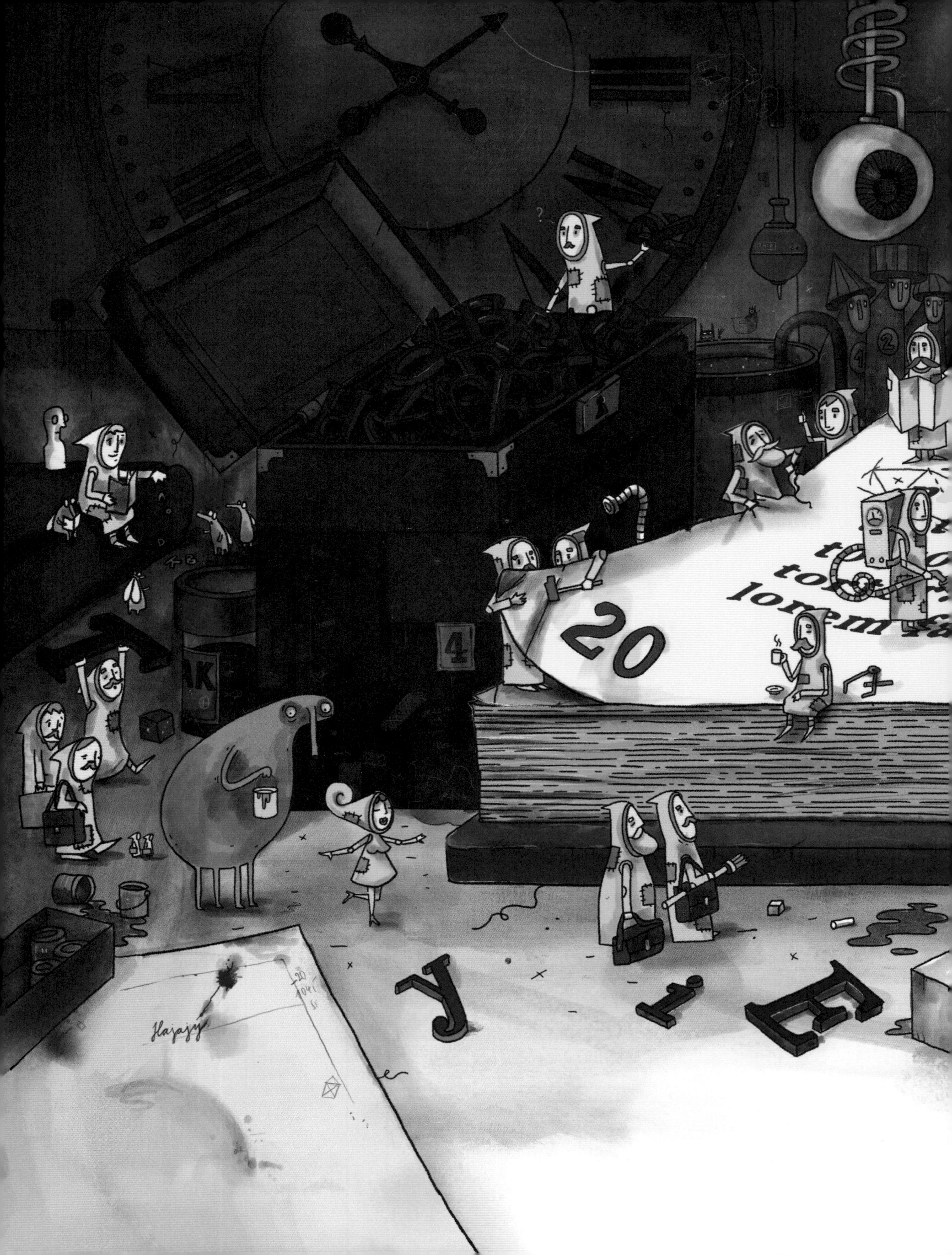
20
4

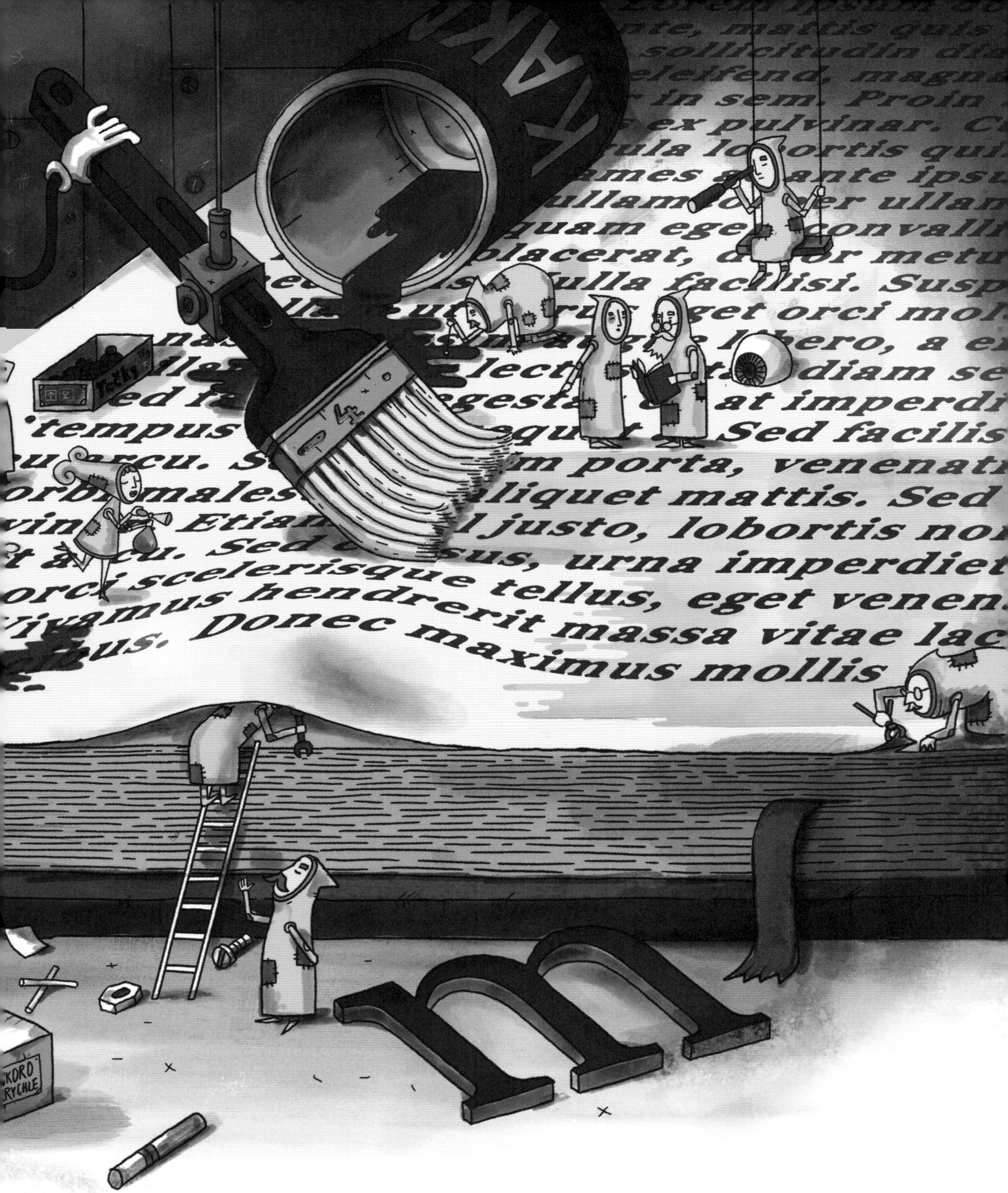

ex pulvinar.
placerat,
Nulla facilisi.
lecti
diam se
at imperdi
tempus
Sed facilis
porta, venenati
aliquet mattis. Sed
justo, lobortis no
urna imperdiet
orci scelerisque tellus, eget venen
hendrerit massa vitae lac
Donec maximus mollis

4: My Sk

friend

im

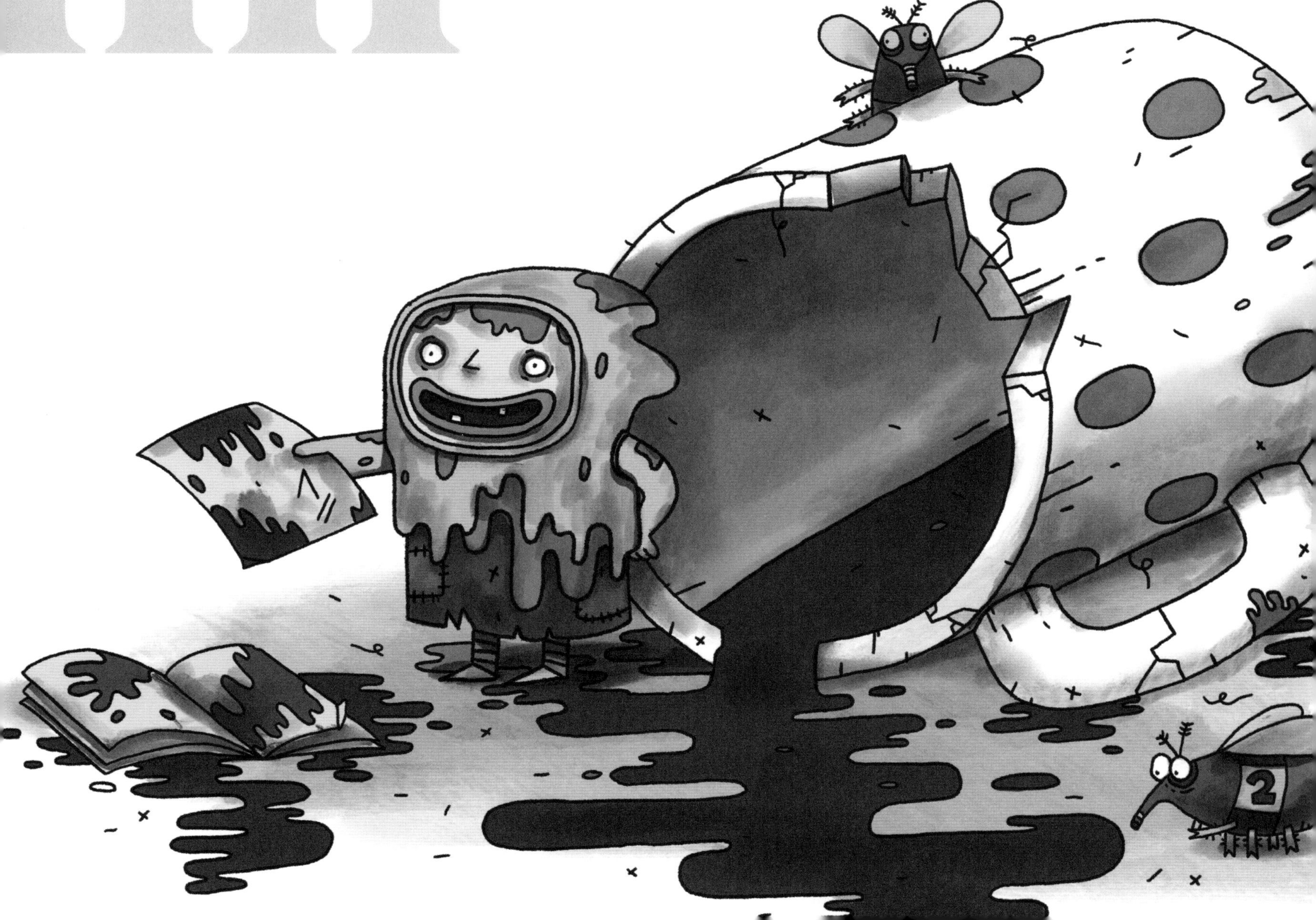
2

Skim and I have been best friends since first grade. No one else wanted to sit next to him, so I did – I felt a bit sorry for him, you see. Skim is terrifically keen on cocoa, and as he leaves a trail wherever he goes, he's a real favorite with the teachers, who keep telling us to follow his shining example. Mrs Frosting, our splotch construction teacher, is always saying that Skim could teach us other entropic elves a thing or two. She refers to his super-messy desk as the model for the rest of us to follow, and to his exercise books and textbooks as the grimiest in the class. You can see for yourself how soiled this page is. That's Skim's work: he loves to read about himself over and over again. The table manners Skim demonstrates in the cafeteria are held up for our admiration, too. But this may surprise you: Skim hates all this praise and attention – he considers himself a rebel; not a teacher's pet.

COARSE DUSTCLUMP (COCONIS VULGARIS)

ORNAMENTAL PLANT THAT PLACES MODEST DEMANDS ON THE CULTIVATOR AND IS ABUNDANT ALL OVER THE WORLD. PECULIAR FOR ITS INTOLERANCE TO WATERING; INDEED, WATER IS HARMFUL TO IT. THRIVES IN DRY, NEVER-WASHED NOOKS. IN POPULAR USE FOR THE CULTIVATION OF ALLERGIES. OFFENSIVELY RECOMMENDED FOR THE AESTHETIC IMPROVEMENT OF NEW AND SHINY SURFACES.

Skim's family runs a stains and mold farm. Only his Uncle Bore is excused work on the farm, because he's terrifically rich from the hours and hours he spends deep underground doing something with oil. It's pretty good on the farm. More than anything, I like to wander the huge plantations where coarse dustclump is grown. These tufts of dust are the ones that form in the corners of rooms and under beds. You have the Skim family to thank for them. Dustclump is brilliant for fooling around with. We used to play at the farm quite often, but Skim's mom started complaining that we were scaring away the moths, so now we go there less.

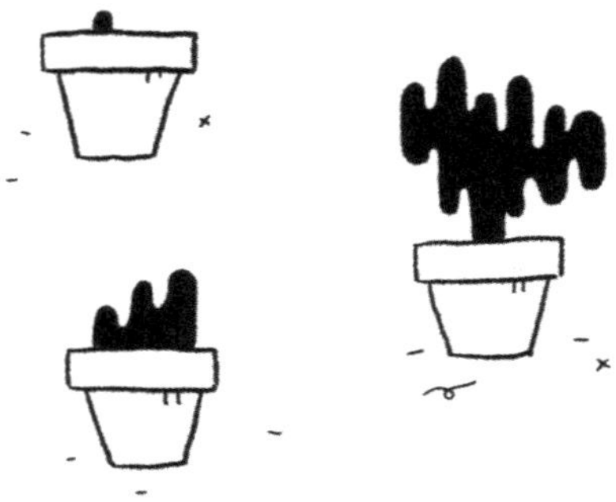

GROWTH OF COMMON STAINER SEEDLINGS

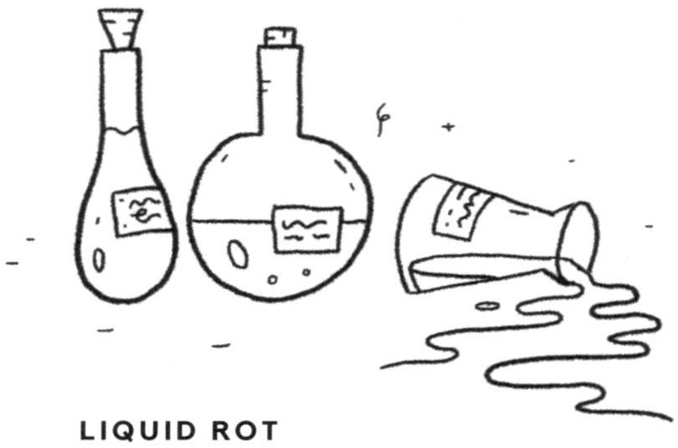

LIQUID ROT

100% CONCENTRATE. DILUTE WITH MOUSE URINE. STORE IN A DAMP, DARK PLACE. ADD POOP IF NECESSARY.

Anyway, Skim and I make a pretty good team. Whenever I need to make a real mess at home, I bring him in for a visit and the job's done in no time. And when I took him to my dad's work once, all his colleagues were mightily impressed with Skim for making a mess of a book within seconds of picking it up. Sometimes I get a bit jealous of this gift of his. But the best thing about Skim is that he never lets it go to his head. Quite the opposite, in fact – he'd bend over backwards for a friend, his kind, messy heart is so big! But one thing he's dreadful at is English. And this is something I can help him with. Typo is my first name and Grammatical Mistakes should be my middle name, so sometimes I do Skim's homework for him. Not long ago we were given a dictation exercise, and as Skim didn't have a single mistake in his, we switched papers. The teacher realized what we'd done, of course: Skim's work was dotted with cocoa stains. Mr Blunder punished us by keeping us in after school to write typos into bus timetables – tedious work, I can tell you!

Although Skim and I get into all kinds of mischief, neither of us would ever leave the other in the lurch. Never ever! Best friends should always watch out for each other. And best friends are what Skim and I have always been and always will be. Except for during that unfortunate incident with the Cog of Time, which I swear I'm slowly getting to. But before I do, let me tell you more about our school...

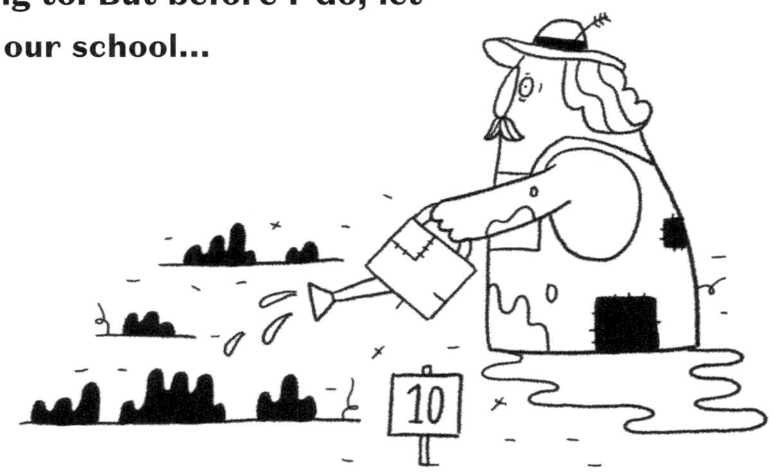
10

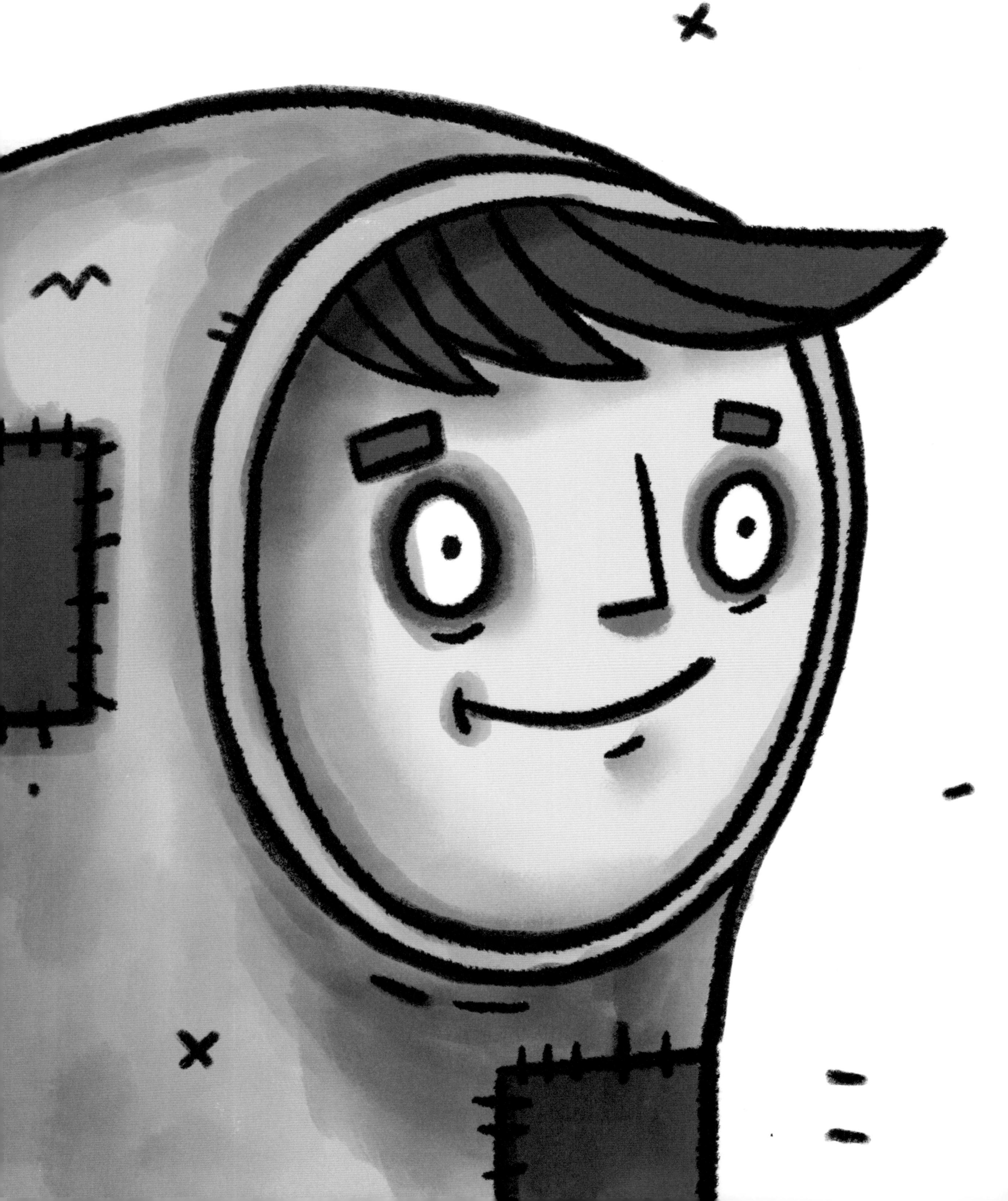

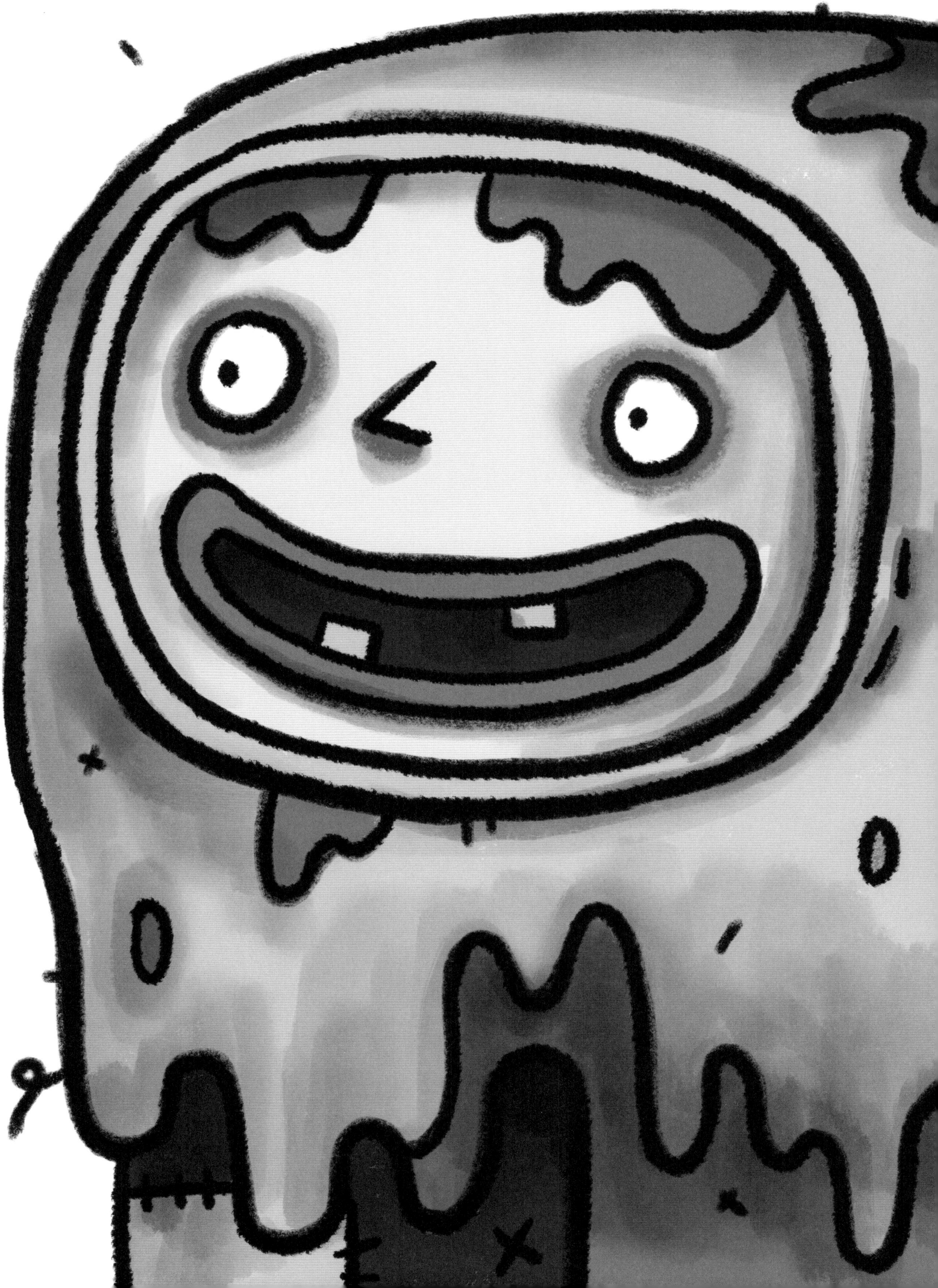

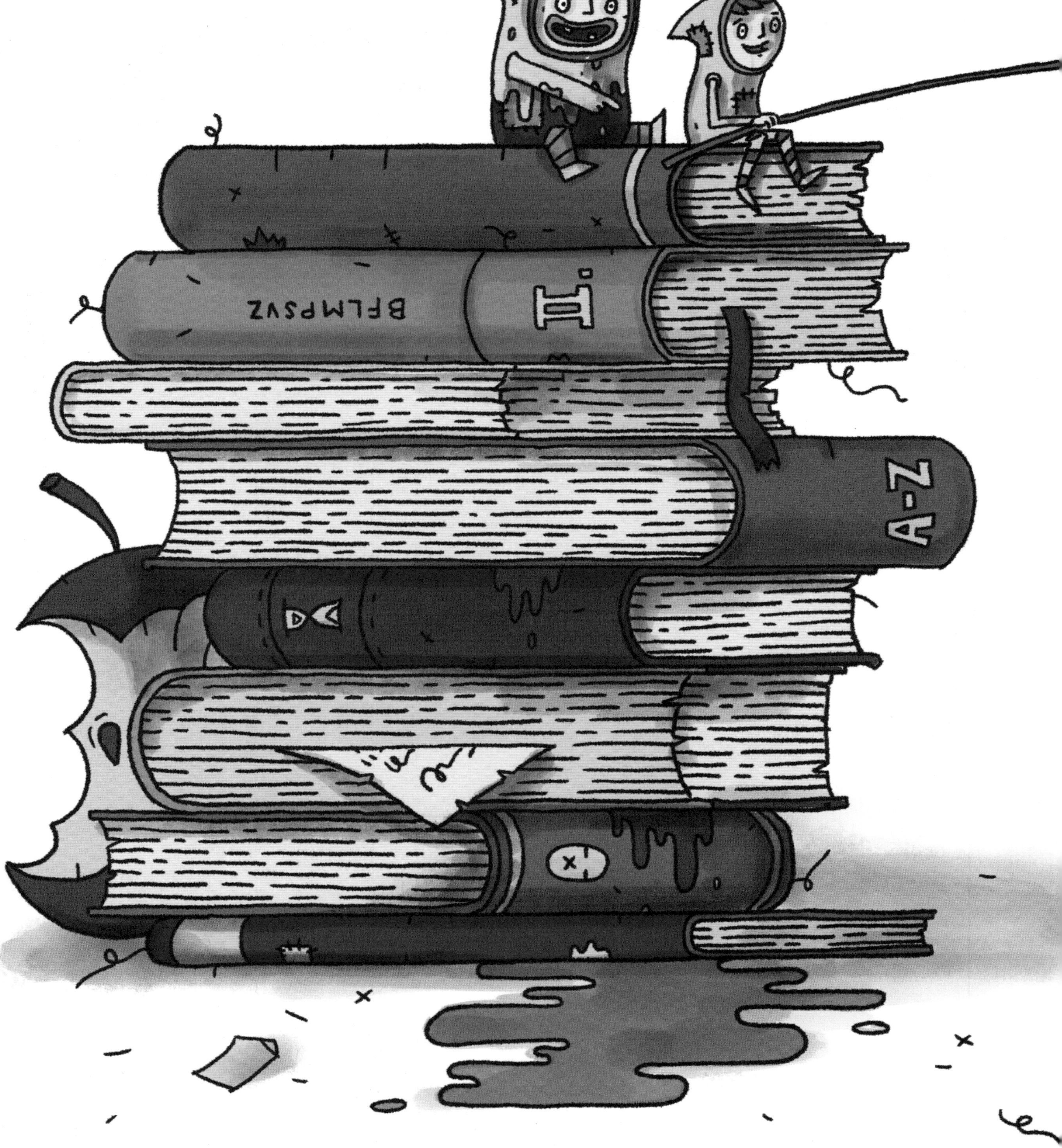

BFLMPSVZ
A-Z

I PROMISE TO WORK
DILIGENTLY AND CONSCIENTIOUSLY
DAY AND NIGHT TO ENSURE THAT
THINGS AGE AND ARE RULED
BY CHAOS.

NOTHING SHOULD EVER REMAIN
WELL ORDERED AND IN ONE PLACE.
EVERYTHING MUST BE DIRECTED
CONSTANTLY TOWARDS ENDLESS
CHAOS AND ENTROPY.

ONLY IF THIS IS SO
WILL OUR UNIVERSE AND WORLD
REMAIN IRRESISTIBLY AWESOME.
O LY IN THIS WAY WILL I BECOME
A TRUE ENTROPIC ELF.

N

PSAT GRADUATE'S SOLEMN VOW

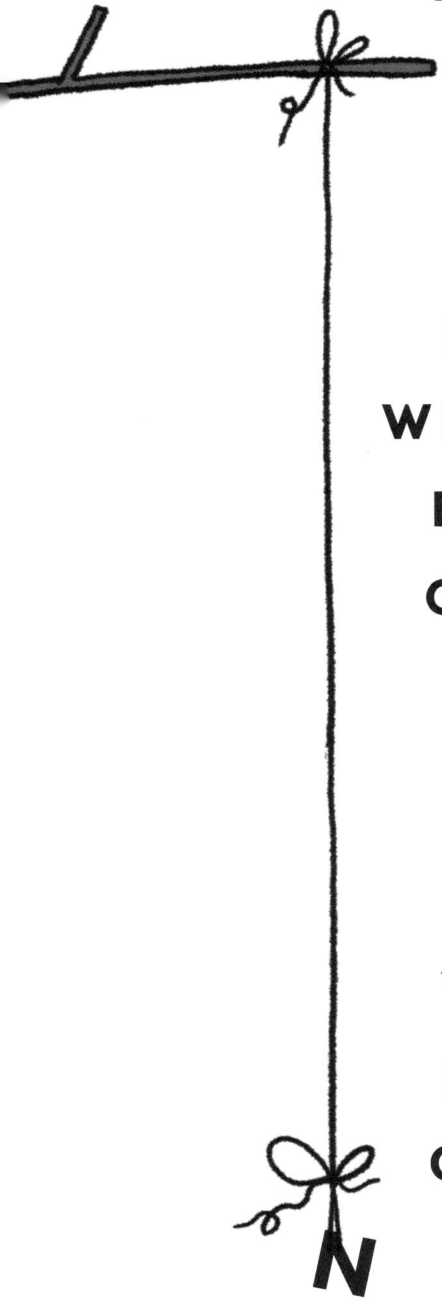

5: Pri
Scho
Ag
Thi

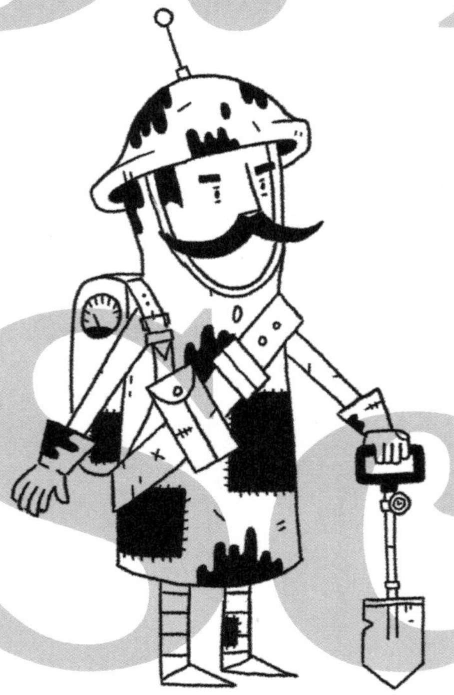

PARATROOPER'S UNIFORM

'NEWT' MODEL, UNISEX, SIZE L,
PERFORATED RUBBER-GUM ELASTIC

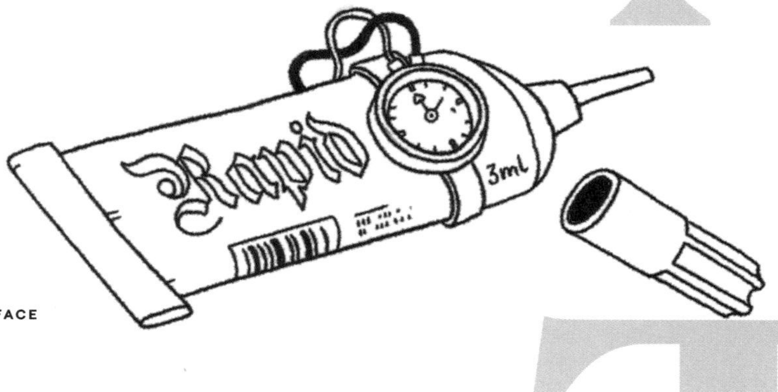

Rapid
3ml

INSTANT UNGLUE

EXTREMELY QUICK-MOISTENING MODEL,
RELIABLY NON-STICK ON ANY KNOWN SURFACE

As I mentioned, Skim and I were in the third grade of the Primary School for Aging Things. The best of us will become paratroopers who venture into the human world. I was really looking forward to seeing the human world. I always imagined it as this huge place filled with things that are aging beautifully. I could hardly wait to become a paratrooper and get my first look at the outside world. But before an entropic elf can achieve such a thing, he must complete his education, plus a thorough (i.e. tedious) program of practical training. Being so small, entropic elves are invisible to humans, but this doesn't mean there aren't safety hazards when we're among them: we must learn how not to get breathed in, stepped on or otherwise squished. Not long ago, our class received a visit from a paratrooper called Mr Soaker, who told us about his work outside in the fountains and water pipes. He was quite a hotshot.

"I'm the head foreman at the fountain quarry," Mr Soaker explained, while the rest of us, especially our teacher Mrs Frosting, listened admiringly. "We break off the calcium deposits required to block drainage outlets. It's dangerous work. Can't be performed without protective headgear. Water can be surprisingly hard."

"Ha! Ha! Hard water indeed! That dude's got a screw loose!" These comments came from the back of the room, where Wormold and Badegg were sitting. These two had arrived in our class in reverse: from the fifth grade via the fourth. They were always causing problems. Mrs Frosting glared at them, but Mr Soaker flowed on: "Gunkers lay special algae on the fountain bed. They use suction cups to stop themselves from slipping and injuring themselves. Caution! humans are in the odd habit of throwing money into fountains. Dodging a dropping coin is a matter of life and death."

"Heads you win. Tales I lose!" giggled Badegg.

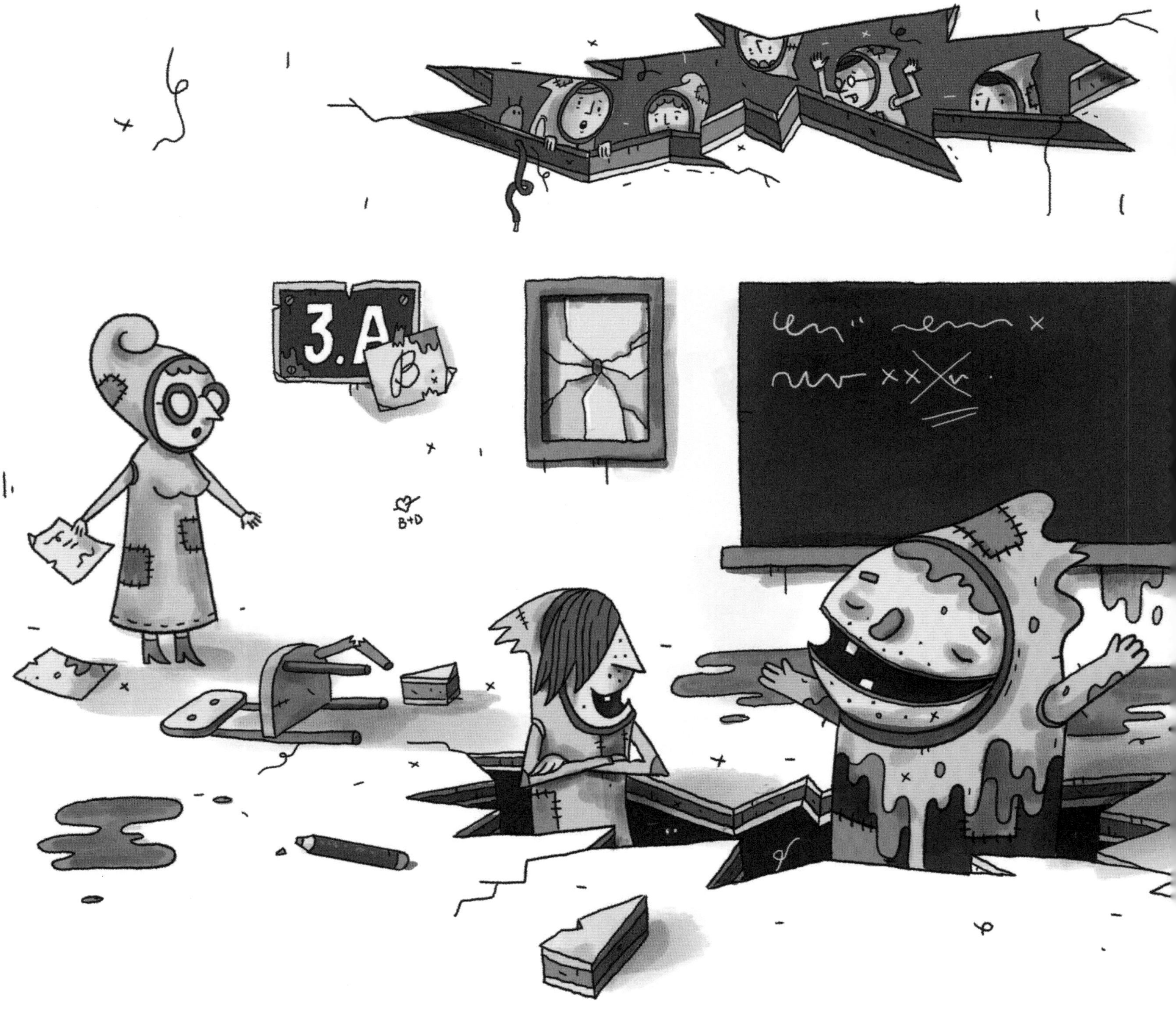
3.A
B+D

"May I ask why your fingers are so lovely and green?" piped up Pryer, who sits right at the front of the class and is curious about everything. "He constantly picks his nose!" guessed Wormold, and Badegg laughed so hard he farted. Mrs Frosting snapped at them that unless they piped down right now, she would send them to the staff-room, where they would be put to work unsticking super glue.

'TP'- PARATROOPER'S BACKPACK WITH TELEPORT AND IN-BUILT METER →

PRIMITIVE APPARATUS FOR RAPID TRANSPORTATION IN SPACE, WHICH WORKS ON THE ATOMIC NUCLEUS/ SNEEZE PRINCIPLE. AN ESSENTIAL TOOL FOR EVERY PARATROOPER. FOR MANY YEARS, IT WAS WRONGLY ASSUMED THAT ITS INVENTOR WAS AMATEUR PHYSICIST AND CONJURER LUDWIG BLUFF. NOW WE KNOW THAT THE PRINCIPLE BEHIND IT WAS DISCOVERED BY BLUFF'S GRANDMOTHER ULRIKE, IN THE PROCESS OF MAKING QUINCE JAM.

Turning to Pryer, Mr Soaker explained: "That's from working with the algae, darling. Every day we take it to our Cosmetic Department for lengthening and dyeing. If you do this job for a long time, the green dye soaks right into you. By the way, this is where the human legend about the so-called waterboy comes from." "Cocoa-loco!" gasped Skim. Now Mrs Frosting was glaring at him. The paratrooper cast his eyes about the room before asking: "Do you know how to recognize a really good fountain, kids?" "No!" we cried in unison. "Is it completely green?" answered Mrs Frosting shyly. "We can tell a good fountain by the fact that there's no water in it," said Mr Soaker triumphantly. "The crowning achievement of our work on a fountain is the stoppering of its jets. I don't like to brag, but we in our department are really fast workers, so you'll find dry fountains in lots of towns. And I can promise you more to come!"

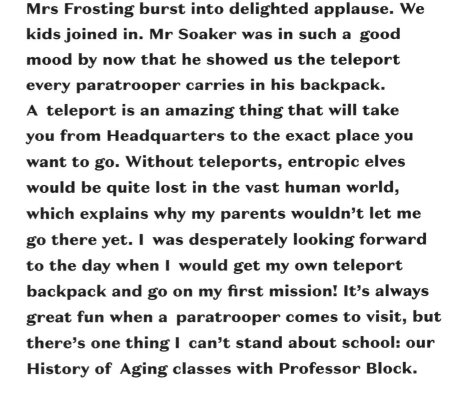

Mrs Frosting burst into delighted applause. We kids joined in. Mr Soaker was in such a good mood by now that he showed us the teleport every paratrooper carries in his backpack. A teleport is an amazing thing that will take you from Headquarters to the exact place you want to go. Without teleports, entropic elves would be quite lost in the vast human world, which explains why my parents wouldn't let me go there yet. I was desperately looking forward to the day when I would get my own teleport backpack and go on my first mission! It's always great fun when a paratrooper comes to visit, but there's one thing I can't stand about school: our History of Aging classes with Professor Block.

6: A

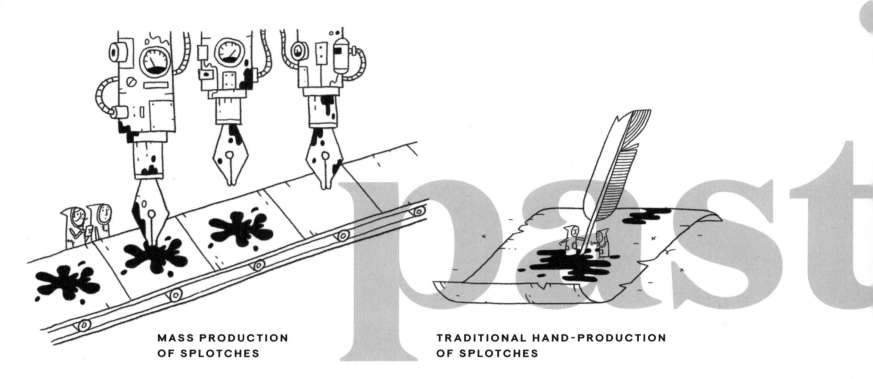

**MASS PRODUCTION
OF SPLOTCHES**

**TRADITIONAL HAND-PRODUCTION
OF SPLOTCHES**

pre

DR PIGMENT

HER INVENTION OF THE SPLOTCH HAS MADE AN INDELIBLE
IMPRESSION ON THE HISTORY OF LITERATURE.

Professor Block is at least 600 years old. Rumor has it that he authored the world's very first printing error. He's the principal at our school. In his classes, we learn about how things have aged from prehistoric times to the present day, discuss the most famous ruins and find out about our celebrated ancestors. If it sounds a little dry, it is. If it was up to me, I'd never go to another history lesson, but my dad insists I do. "Listen carefully to what Professor Block tells you," he says. "He's a real expert! What he doesn't know about aging, isn't worth knowing. And just remember – a curious mind ages quickest!" That's one of my dad's favorite sayings. You see, among entropic elves, nobody takes you seriously unless you're at least a hundred...

In the foreword to the omnibus edition of Professor Block's Aging in History: Volumes I – MDCCCXVII, we can read the following: "Above all it is necessary to realize that the things around you were not always old and battered.

MANUAL TWO-SIDED HOLE PUNCH WITH SAFETY CATCH

CAUTION: REQUIRES EXTREMELY CAREFUL HANDLING. KEEP OUT OF REACH OF PERSONS YOUNGER THAN 100 YEARS. NEVER USE WITHOUT THE SAFETY CATCH. NEVER, EVER!

"The universe, too, was once new, sweet-smelling and shiny, but fortunately that changed when the Cog of Time appeared. Since then, the principle of *fugit irreparabile tempus* – that's Latin for time flies irretrievably – has applied. For it to produce the fruits of aging we desire, it's necessary that we keep up with it. From its very beginnings, our history is bound up with the history of humankind. Since Old Father Drrrrng etched the first scratch, our ancestors have worked tirelessly to ensure that everything on Earth ages. The Neanderthal entropic used only primitive tools, just like their humanoid counterparts. Nevertheless, these formed the basis of modern tools. Yesterday's flint blunter and bone-trowel hole punch developed into today's modern nibbler and remote-controlled road crimper!

"We take most pride in the monuments of Ancient Egypt, Greece and Rome. Even humans have always admired how splendidly faded and battered they are; thanks in part to these ruins the tourism industry was born. Unfortunately, we still come across humans who show no understanding for our work – I am referring to the groups of 'vandals' known as restorers and conservators. By their efforts to repair and renovate these monuments or restore them to their original condition, these humans undermine the difficult, meticulous work that entropic elves have devoted to them over many, many years. How very barbaric!"

Phew – and that's just the foreword! You really don't want to know what he writes about after that.

Our History of Aging lessons drift like the Cog of Time has stopped: half the class sleeps while Wormold and Badegg play a game of wrecks at their desk at the back; Professor Block stands at the board like a ghost, and we have to write down every word he says. He explains in excruciating detail how Dr Pigment designed the first splotch, or how the Ripz brothers invented technology for the unraveling of fabrics. He also makes us learn, by heart and in its entirety, Dr Strangestuff's periodic table of staining elements. The worst assignment ever was an essay with the title: "Which came first, the chicken or the egg?" I flailed away at that for about a month! Try to answer it yourself. Go on. It's impossible! And do you know why? Block finally revealed it's the oldest question in the world that no one has ever found an answer to. Does it even make sense? It goes on and on. The best fun we had with it was when Badegg claimed that, when an egg hatches, the chicken that comes out of it is actually a spoiled egg. He and Block argued for ages about this.

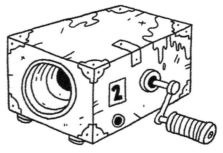

NIBBLER

FOR THE FIRST NIBBLING OF UNNIBBLED OR THE FINAL NIBBLING OF WELL-NIBBLED PENCILS

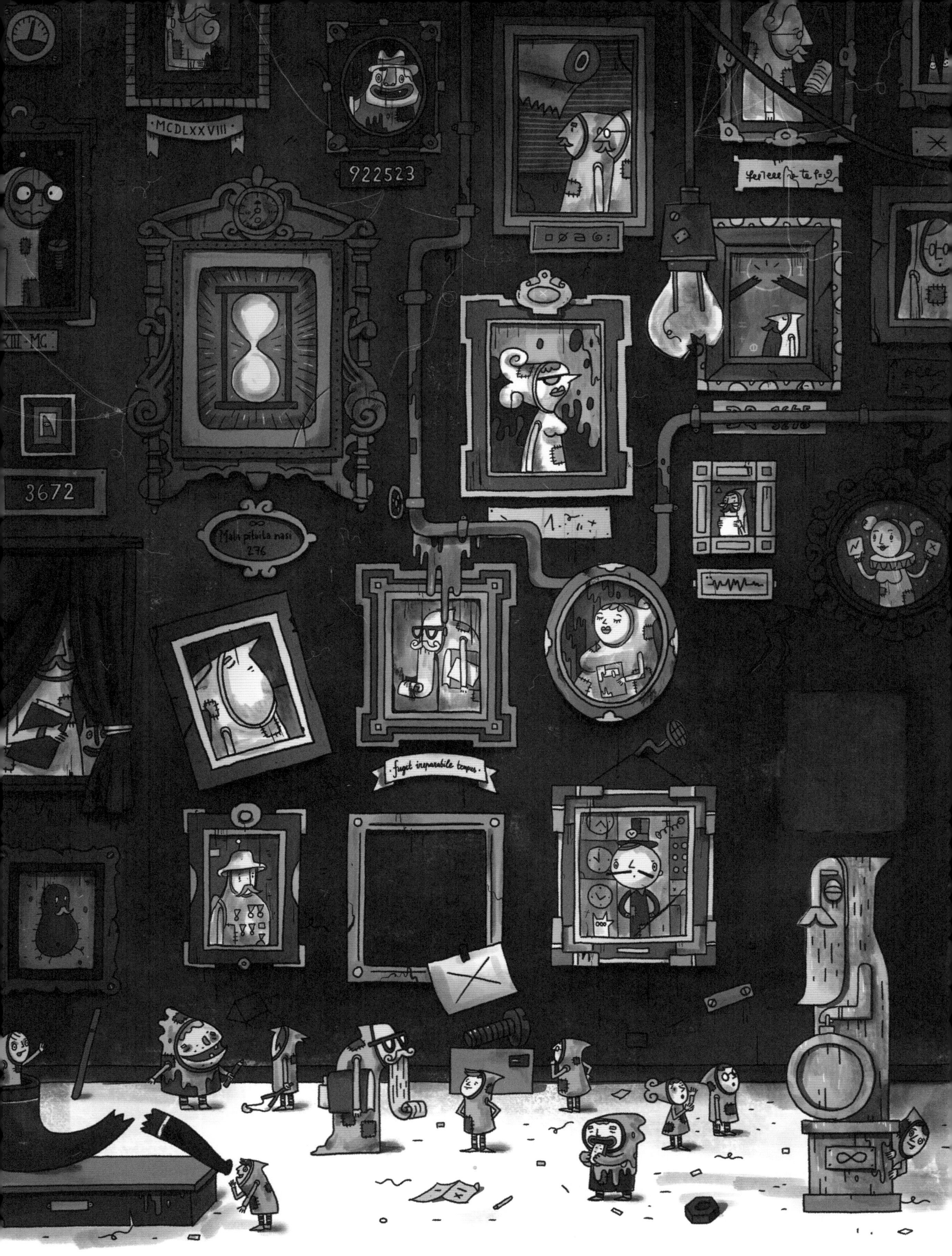
MCDLXXVIII
922523
3672
Mali pibila nasi
276
fugit ireparabile tempus

In my view, the History of Aging is quite simply
the most pointless subject in the world. I believe
that the entropic elves of old did what they
could, of course. But I also think that the best
period for aging is the one we live in now! Just
look at how incredibly quickly the objects and
appliances in your home age. All the washing
machines, fridges, television sets, cars – even
your toys; never before has aging occurred
at such speed. We see it most clearly with
computers and mobile phones, some of which
last barely six months, and then you have
to buy a new one. Isn't it great?!

If there's one thing at school that's really cool, it's the
lab for new aging technologies. Unfortunately, we won't
get to use it until we're in the fifth grade, but we have
been given a tour of it, which I really enjoyed. This is the
place where modern-classic inventions like instant unglue
and the unsafety pin come from. Lab work includes the
tangling of nanofibres and the blinding of optical fibres,
and instruments include a giant particle retardant. A large
section of the lab is given over to plastics decomposition
technologies, an area where we haven't had much success
so far. Even the best corrodant takes at least fifty years
to make any kind of impact on a PET bottle.

What interests me most, though, is the
Computer Department, which works on viruses
and program errors. When I was there, they
let me write something on the latest model of
an obsolete touch keyboard, and I have to say
that I've never found it easier to make typos.
So much for Dad's rewriting of books by hand!

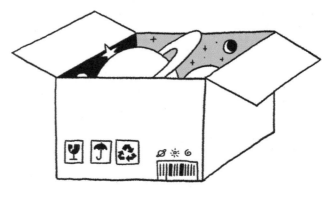

UNIVERSE 1.0

THIS SIDE UP. KEEP UPRIGHT. FRAGILE. BEST BEFORE – SEE
PACKAGING

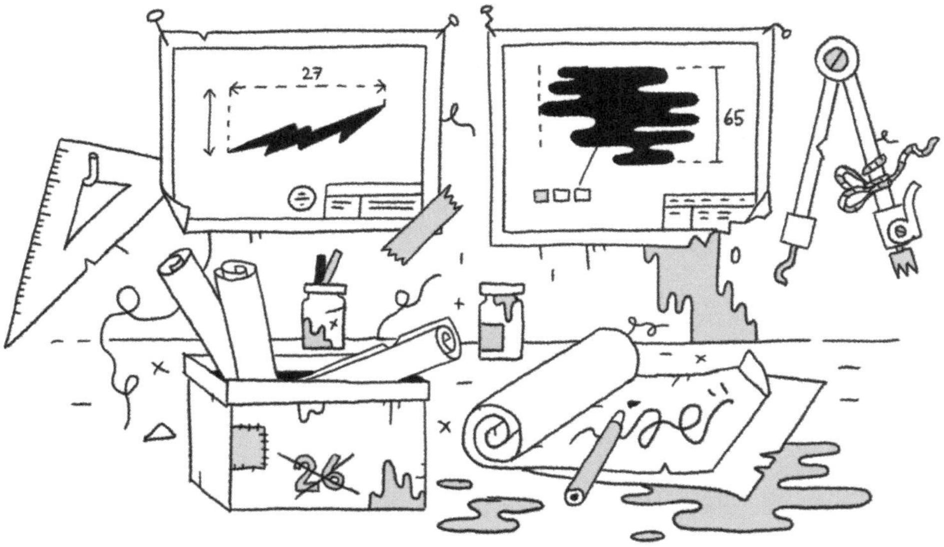
27
65
26

ENGINEERING DESIGN OFFICE FOR MASS-PRODUCED SCRATCHES

A TYPICAL SCENE IN THE DEPARTMENT FOR THE DAMAGE TO NEW SURFACES. "A SCRATCH COMBINES THE NATURAL BEAUTY OF THE SWIPE OF A TIGER'S PAW WITH STATE-OF-THE-ART TECHNOLOGIES. WHENEVER I COME ACROSS A PERFECTLY EXECUTED SCRATCH, WHAT ELSE CAN I DO BUT SCRATCH MY HEAD IN WONDER AT HOW IT WAS ACHIEVED?"

VALERIE TATTERSALL, POET AND LOVER OF LIFE

Dad hates the laboratory, of course, claiming that new technologies take work from entropic elves by making the process of decomposition faster and easier. When I told him about the chrono pressure suit, he got really, really angry. You put this suit on when you want to place yourself totally beyond the Cog of Time. Its inventor, Dr Littlehand, told us that whoever puts on the suit can control time using a temporegulator or whatever it's called.

The problem is, Dr Littlehand and his team in the Department for the Flow of Time have been working on the chrono pressure suit for an awfully long time and still it isn't quite ready or properly tested. On top of that, nobody really understands the point of it. Dad says that it's unnatural: entropic elves have always cooperated with the Cog of Time, and besides, it's not right to interfere with the Cog of Time and aging. Although Dr Littlehand was nominated for the Crystal Zilch award for his pressure suit, in the end it went to Skim's Uncle Remoudou for his work at the dump. Which was fine by me, as it meant I finally got to attend the Crystal Zilch awards ceremony.

7: Cr
Zil

MAURICE'S GLEAMING TROPHIES

1 100M DUNG RUN CHAMPION

2 200M² DUNG RUN CHAMPION

3 FAR-FLUNG DUNG RUN CHAMPION

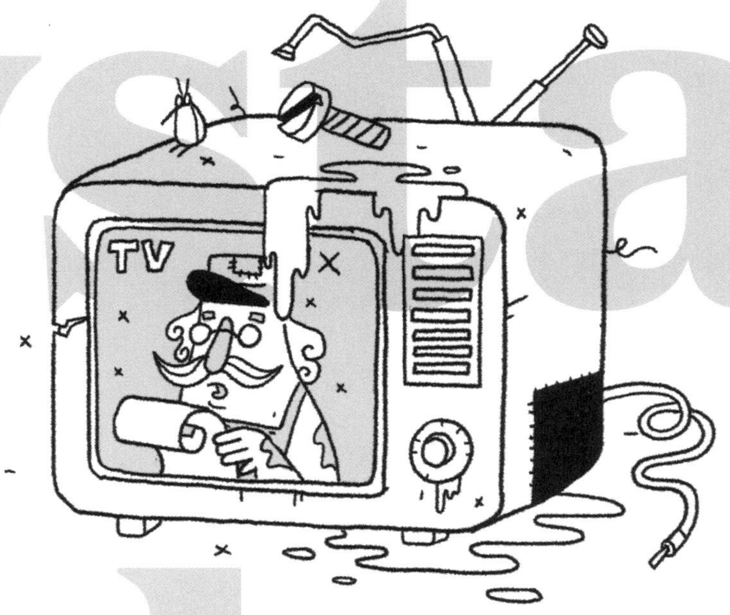
TV

Every year the Crystal Zilch aging awards are conferred at a magnificent ceremony. My parents never want to attend what they think is a really snobbish affair – they're quite happy to watch the whole thing on television. But this year I was in luck; Skim got a free ticket – not just for him, but for me as well – from his uncle, Remoudou.

Skin's Uncle Remoudou, who works at the dump, is a pretty good guy. Wherever he goes, his tame dung beetle Maurice goes with him. Since winning Maurice in a game of cards, he's taught him to pull the peelings cart. "Ahem, this ain't any old dung beetle, lads," Remoudou often tells us. "This here is Maurice the triple dung run champion!"

But at the awards ceremony, Remoudou was so nervous at having been nominated for the Crystal Zilch for lifetime achievement in decomposition that he didn't even speak to us. In fact, he was so intent on stroking Maurice's antennae – an attempt to calm his nerves – that he didn't even notice us when we said hi to him.

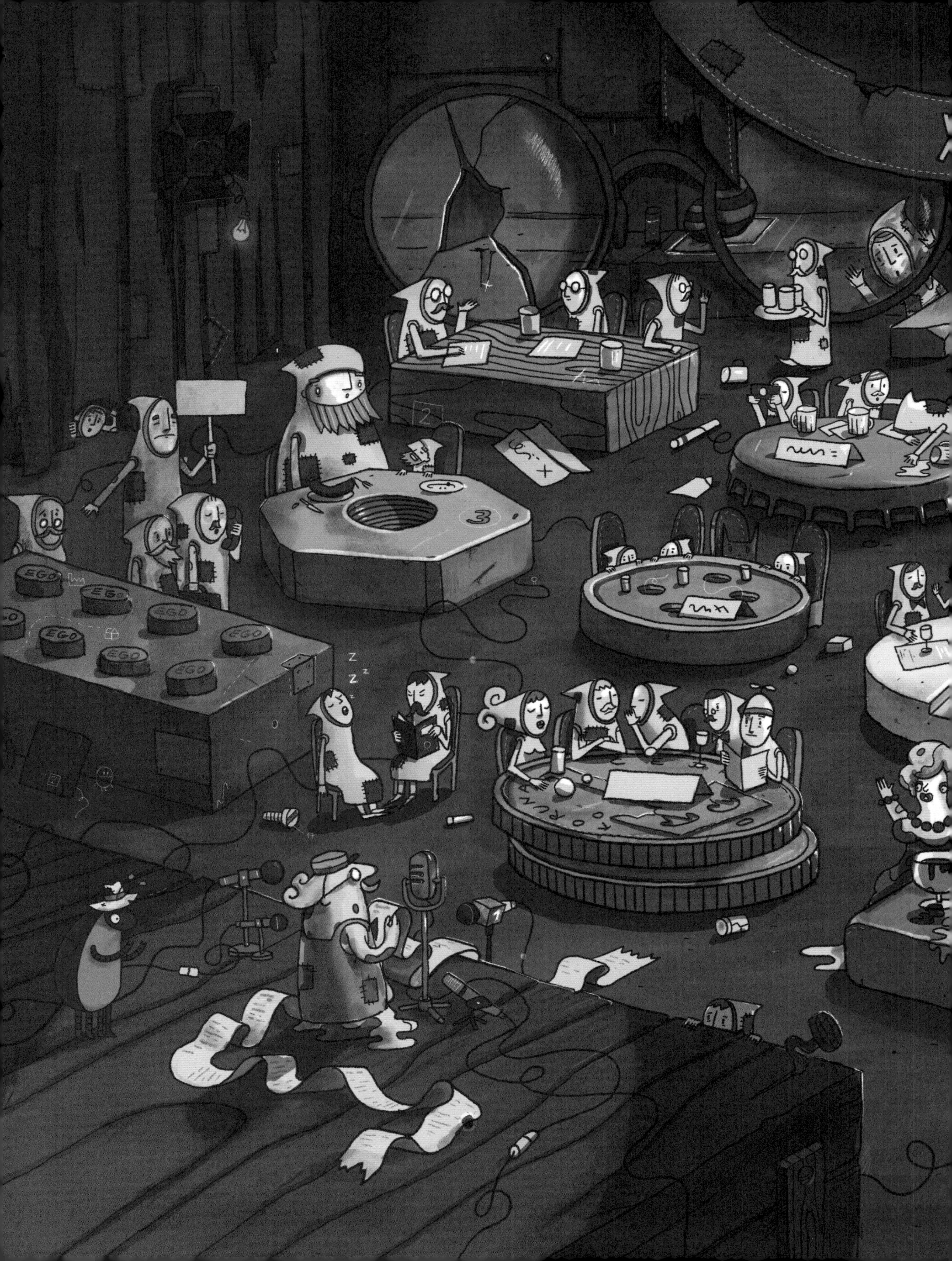
2
3
EGO
KORUNA

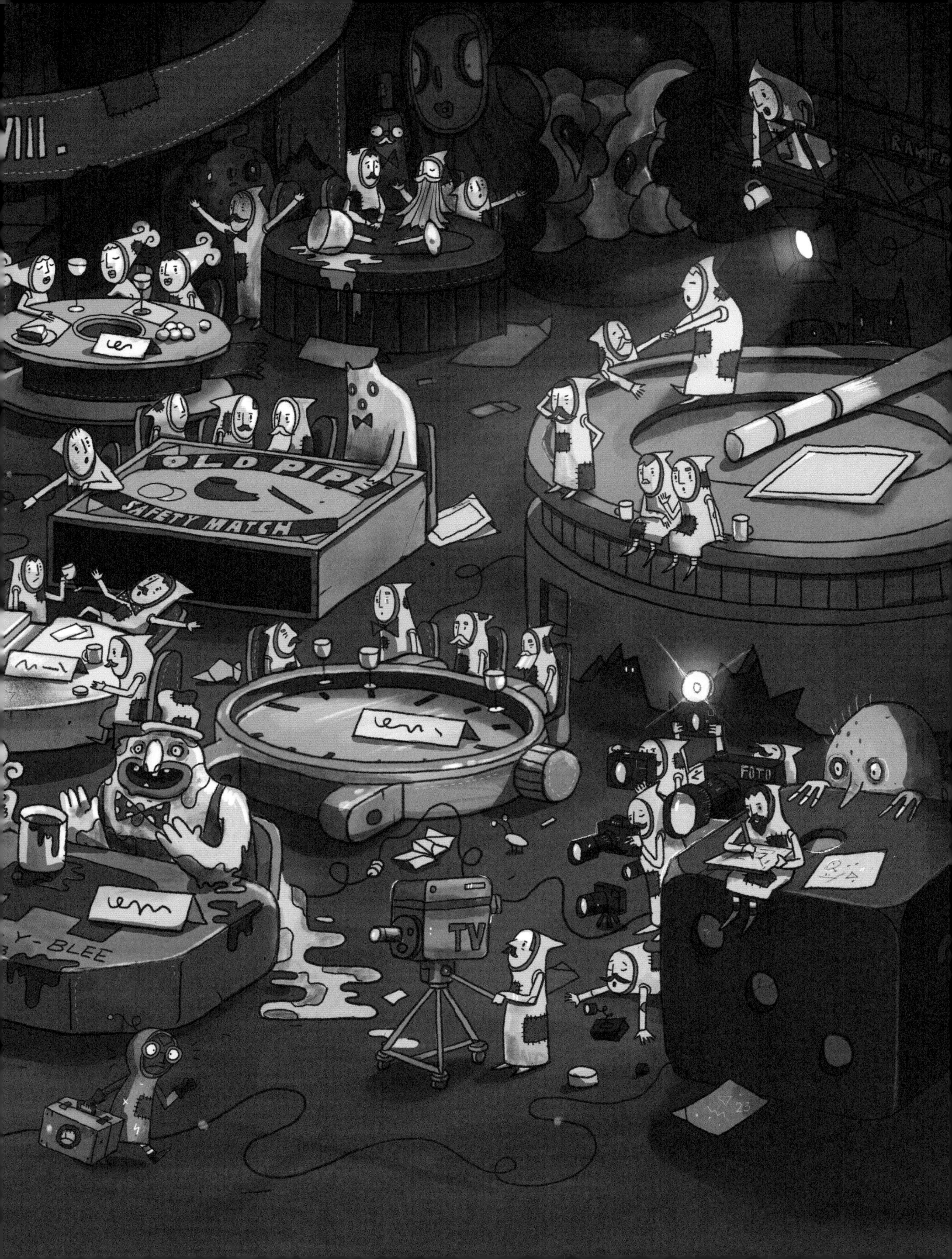
OLD PIPE
SAFETY MATCH
FOTO
TV

This didn't upset me at all, however, as there's always plenty to see at the Zilch awards. It's a who's who of aging, decomposition and disintegration. They pat each other on the back while they gobble stale canapés, sip vinegary wine and make long speeches.

The Skim family had their own table right next to the stage, so my view couldn't have been better. The entropic elves from the Textiles Department sat at the table next to ours. True aces in their field, they make short work of everything. Before you know it, the elbow of your jacket is worn through or a button is hanging off your shirt. Dr Dorsal-Finn, the well-known breeder of flapping shoe soles (known to us as 'sharks'), was sitting very close to me, earnestly explaining something about rot gum.

Behind us sat the match-snappers, the glasses-smudgers, and a couple of gorgeous green elves from the Department of Medicines Past Their Use-by Date. In the middle of the hall I noticed the Department for Sinking Beer Froth; most of those sitting there were asleep with their head on the table. Quite simply, the place was packed, and the wakeful were looking forward to the start of the event.

Before the prizes were conferred, there was a performance by some older students at the PSAT that involved a dishwasher. First, a brand-new dishwasher was brought onto the stage and loaded with brand-new plates, pots and glasses. Then our older classmates pounced on it and proceeded to block the outflow pipe, corrode the nozzles, and soil, scratch, and chip the dishes. In five minutes flat, they made the dishwasher and its contents look like they'd been used by a family of seven for six years.

CRYSTAL ZILCH

"ER… WHAT HAVE I ACTUALLY WON?" BORIS S. BENDER, WINNER OF THE VERY FIRST ZILCH FOR PUCKERING.

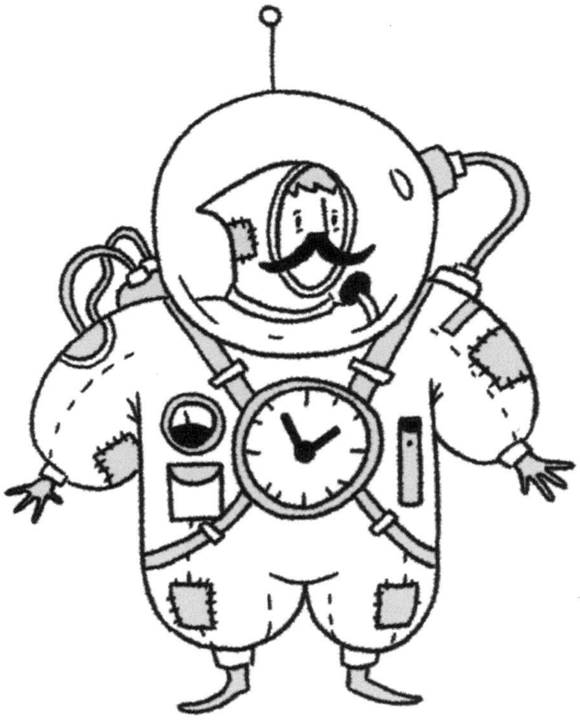

CHRONO PRESSURE SUIT

BREAKTHROUGH INVENTION (AT THAT TIME, REGRETTABLY, STILL WITHOUT PRACTICAL APPLICATION) BY AN ECCENTRIC ENGINEER CALLED LITTLEHAND (WHO, ALSO REGRETTABLY, WAS STILL A ZILCH-FREE ZONE).

Skim was secretly in love with a fifth-grader called Steela who was performing staining tricks on a stainless-steel pan, so he thought it was great. Poor Skim knew that his love could never come to anything, as Steela was as hard as nails, and she couldn't stand the taste of anything sweet, cocoa least of all. When the performance was over, the waiters carried around deliciously stinky refreshments on what was left of the trashed dishes. The winners could be announced at last.

Although I was cheering for Uncle Remoudou along with all Skim's relations, I was keeping a watchful eye on Dr Littlehand, who was sitting at a table at the back, still wondering if he might win a Zilch for his chrono pressure suit after all. But when – as I have led you to expect – Uncle Remoudou was announced as the winner, Dr Littlehand went red, then purple in the face. And while an emotional Uncle Remoudou was getting hugs and slaps on the back from everyone in the audience, including me, Littlehand made straight for the stage with a mysterious briefcase in his hand.

"Listen up!" he boomed into the microphone. The entire room fell silent with surprise. Littlehand cleared his throat before continuing. "To make things absolutely clear, I haven't toiled away my whole life in expectation of a Zilch! If you think a worn-out old stinker like Remodou deserves one more than me, you're welcome to your opinion. Being misunderstood is something geniuses of my distinction learn to live with. That said, I've decided that I shall demonstrate my chrono pressure suit for the very first time in public here and now, on myself!"

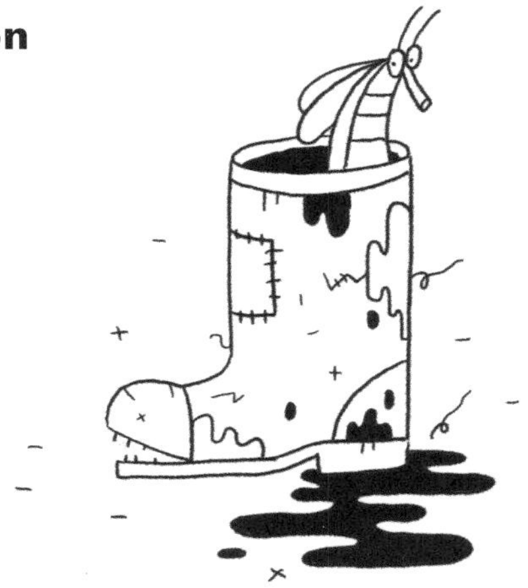

With those words, Littlehand proceeded to haul
his invention from his briefcase. And before
any stunned audience member could stop him,
he donned the pressure suit and proclaimed:
"Either I die, or I change the course of history
forever!" He pressed something inside the suit.
There was a muffled humming and then silence...

Dr Littlehand pressed something else. Silence.
Littlehand went on pressing things. Then he
proceeded to slap the pressure suit, jump up and
down in it comically, stamp and thrash about, and
shout oaths. Finally, he leapt from the stage and
fled the scene, to the sound of rapturous applause
and whistling from the audience. Quite simply,
Dr Littlehand is a lovable eccentric.

He was followed on the stage by Uncle Remoudou
and Maurice, dung beetle extraordinaire.
Remoudou pulled out a super-long list of all the
entropic elves he wished to thank for helping
him get his Zilch. He talked and talked and
talked. I think I dozed off at one point, but I was
awake in time to hear Uncle Remoudou say:

"Ahem. So once again, thank you all very much indeed. Life
at the dump doesn't always smell of roses, as you might
say. Ahem. So I appreciate your help all the more: without
all of you, there wouldn't even be any dump. Before
I finish, above all I'd like to thank my family, who dropped
me off at the dump in good time, making it possible for
me to win this wonderful, ahem, Zilch. It means the world
to me, and I wish everyone whose work falls apart in their
hands as nicely as it does in mine, could have one. Long
live our tireless efforts to make the world a better place!
Long live aging! Long live decay! Viva entropy! Ahem.
Thank you." Applause. This had been a great Zilch awards
show. But the adventure I would have was greater still.

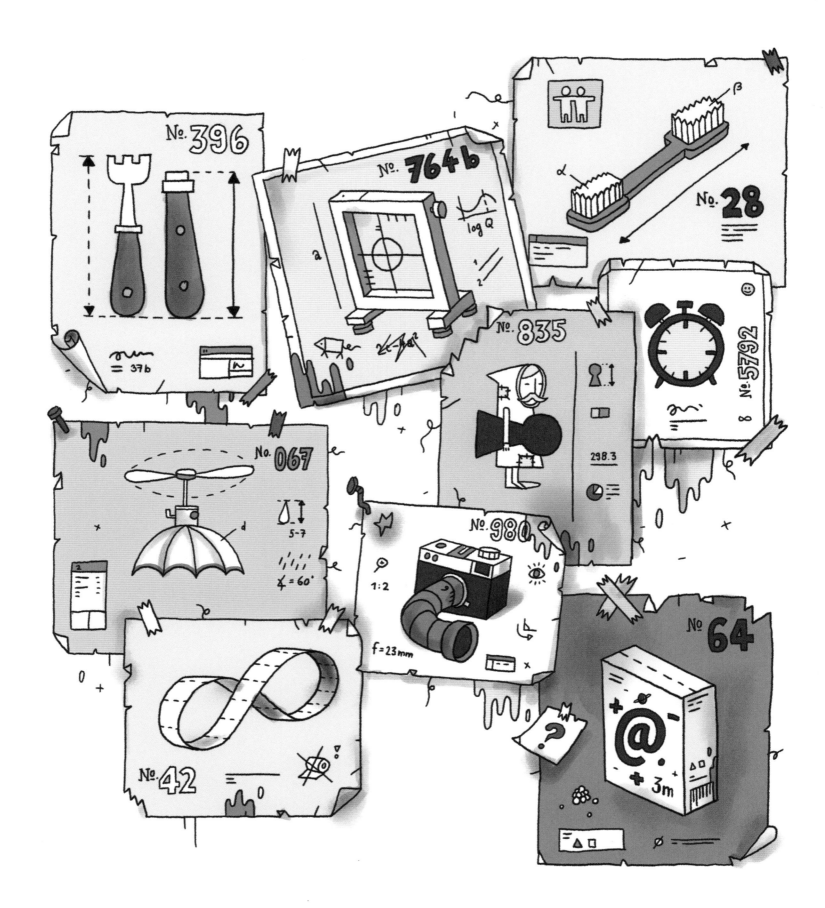

**INGENIOUS INVENTIONS BY THE UNJUSTLY
UNREWARDED DR LITTLEHAND:**

NO. 396 SAFETY CUTLERY

NO. 764B SIGHTING FRAME FOR THE INTERSECTION OF PARALLEL LINES

NO. 835 PORTABLE KEYHOLE

NO. 28 TOOTHBRUSH FOR SIAMESE TWINS

NO. 5792 HANDLESS ALARM CLOCK FOR THE PROLONGING OF LIFE'S FINER MOMENTS

NO. 067 SELF-SUPPORTING UMBRELLA

NO. 980 LENS FOR AROUND-THE-CORNER SHOTS

NO. 42 ENDLESS TOILET PAPER

NO. 64 ANTIMATTER POWDER (FAMILY PACK)

8: T

to

patis

A TRAGIC INCIDENT WITH A GUMMY BEAR

PARATROOPER SIMPLETON WAS TRAPPED INSIDE A GUMMY BEAR WHEN IT HARDENED AS HE WAS ATTEMPTING TO MELT IT. AS A CONSEQUENCE, THIS METHOD OF MELTING WAS ABANDONED FOR SAFETY REASONS.

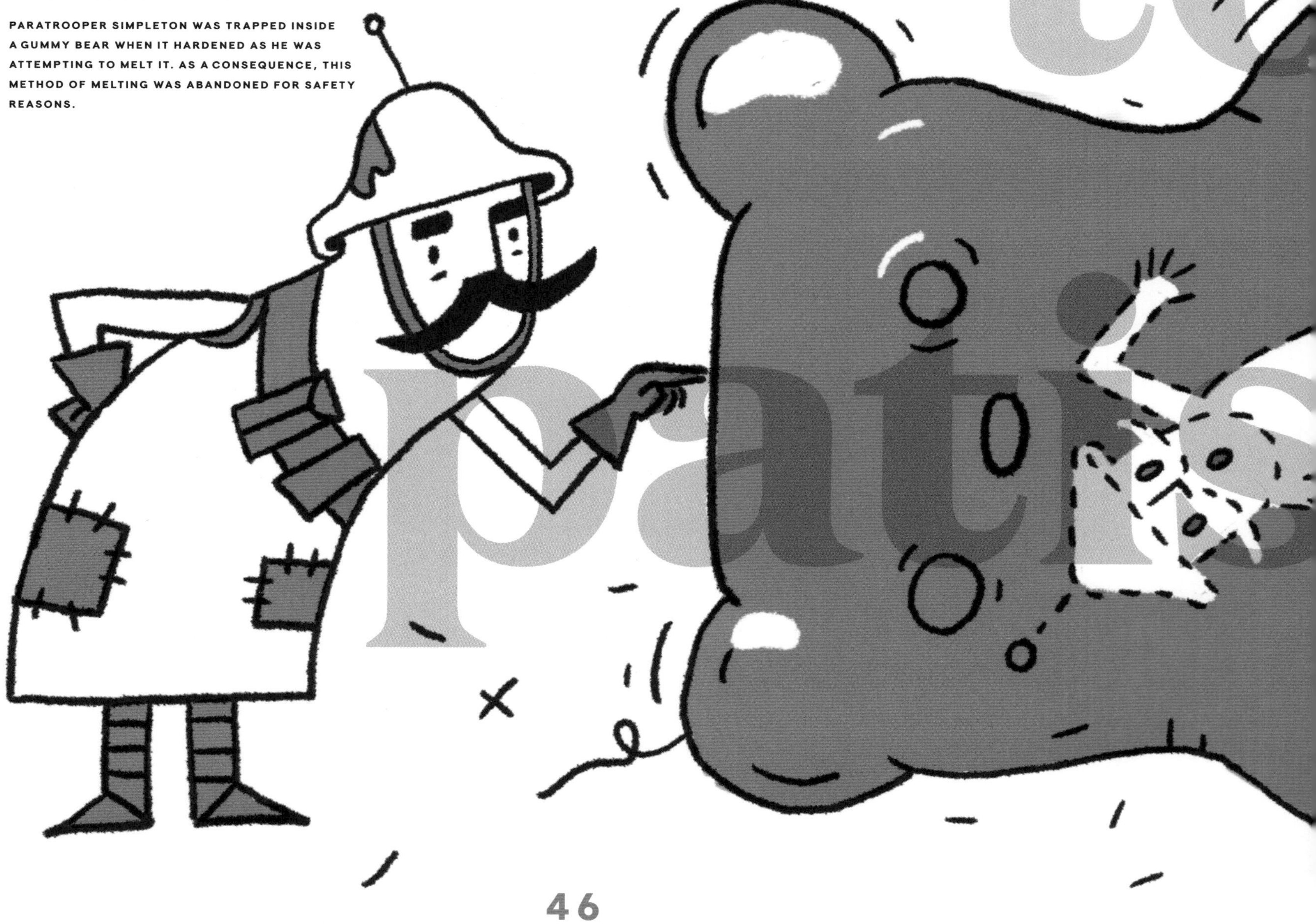

The day my life changed began with Mrs Frosting taking us to a patisserie - a fancy cake shop. I could hardly wait to see the outside world at last. Not only did I look forward to seeing our paratroopers at work, I was burning with curiosity about what humans were like. I wondered how they appreciated what we entropic elves did for them. As we were invisible to them, did they even notice our handiwork? Did it make them glad that everything around them aged? I had tons of questions like this.

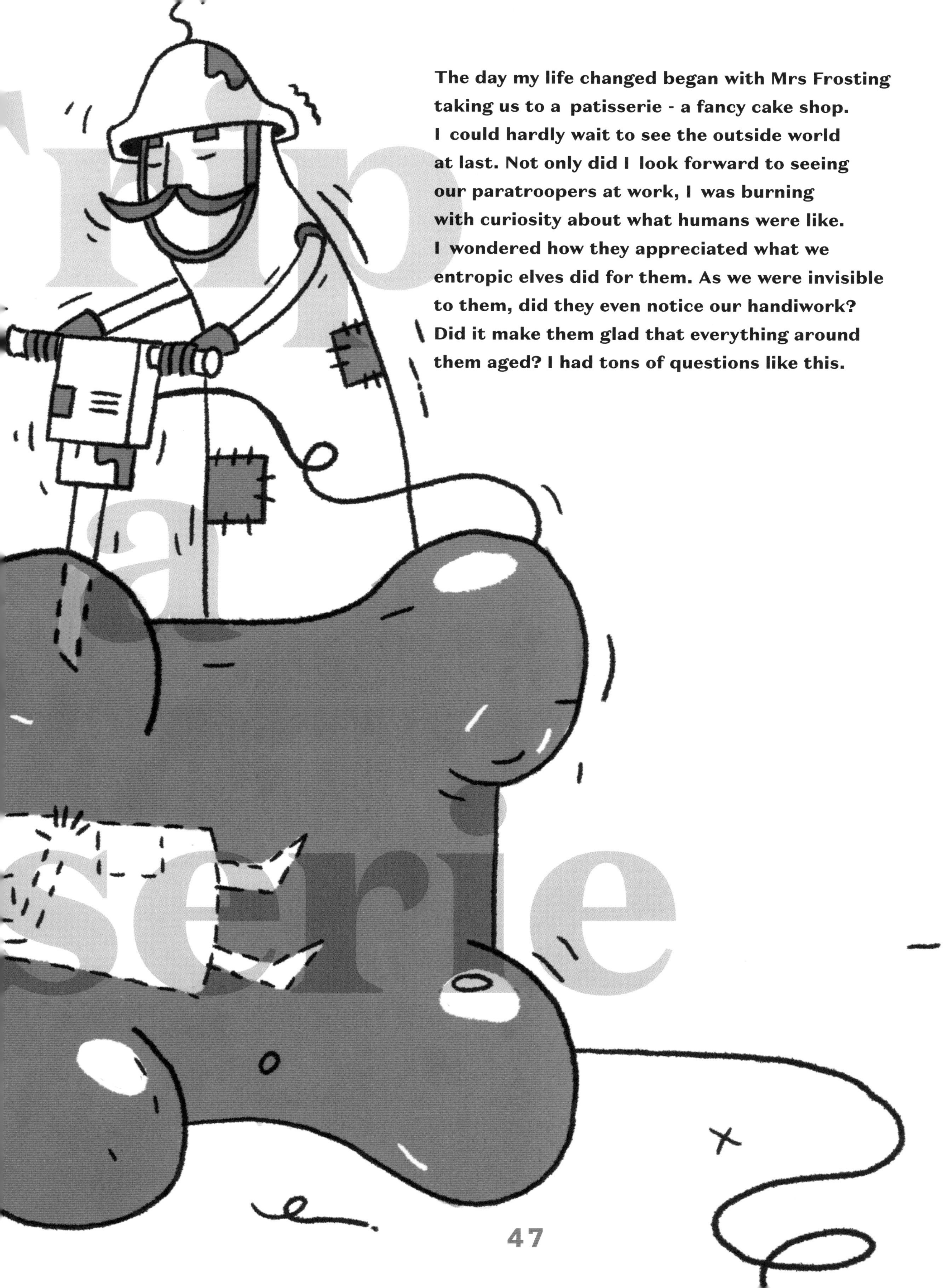

For a sweet-tooth like Skim, of course, a trip to a patisserie was a dream come true, and he had ants in his pants from early morning. Did I think they would they let him put a skim on just one mug of cocoa? he asked me.

Mrs Frosting handed out real paratrooper's teleports to everyone. Badegg and Wormold immediately pressed something on theirs, there was a gentle farting sound, and they disappeared before our very eyes. But Mrs Frosting wasn't having any of it: she pulled out a large walkie-talkie and called them straight back. But in the brief moment the two of them had spent in the patisserie, they had succeeded in stealing some chocolate ice cream, which had melted in teleportation and was now dripping off them. Both claimed to have pressed their teleport by mistake, but Mrs Frosting took their teleports back. Instead of going on the trip, Badegg and Wormold would have to stay in the classroom, making splotches in their exercise books – which absolutely served them right.

After that, everything went like clockwork. We put on our teleport backpacks; then, on Mrs Frosting's command, we pressed the button, there was that gentle farting sound – and – wow! – I found myself in the patisserie.

It was amazing, I can tell you! There we were, on the very top shelf among tarts, cream rolls, lollipops, boiled sweets and many other kinds of goodies, with paratroopers from the Department of Food working on them. Flies and other insects were buzzing around our heads, there were all kinds of beetles and ants staggering about, and besides all this, huge humans kept lumbering into the patisserie to buy sweet things to take home with them. It was enough to make your head spin!

I wasn't the only one whose eyes were bugging out. Skim kept nudging me and pointing at things. "Wow-wee! See those dynamite sweets?" he cried. "And over there – that éclair that looks like a coffin. There's a vampire in it! Cocoa-loco!"

Mrs Frosting called us together by the iced donuts, which a squad of paratroopers was in the process of laboriously undecorating. "Don't go running off, kids," she said in a very loud voice – all the activity in the patisserie made it much noisier there than in the library, for instance.

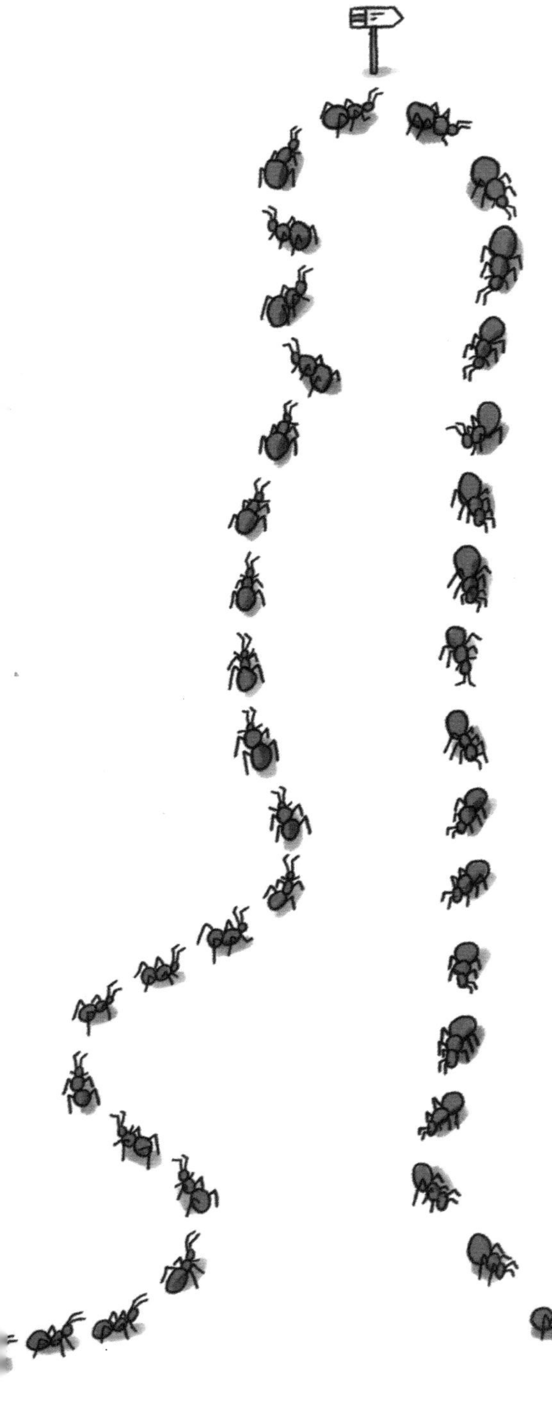

"As you can see," the teacher continued, "this is a vast place and, just because the people can't see us, doesn't mean that it isn't very dangerous for us here. They could easily squash us without even noticing, you know?"

Pryer spoke up to ask if we would be able to try something, like putting holes in a cream roll, but Mrs Frosting shook her head emphatically. "Of course not! That would be too dangerous, children. You can see for yourselves that people are always coming in to buy things. You stop paying attention for just a second and you might find yourself taken to some human's home in a box. Wait here in an orderly fashion for Dr Louse, the insectologist, who will educate us about what goes on a patisserie." We all mumbled our disappointment – the worst thing about field trips was having to listen to another boring talk. Skim muttered something about how much he'd been looking forward to the cocoa, but I didn't pay much attention to him. What Mrs Frosting had said had got me thinking. What about? I'll tell you later.

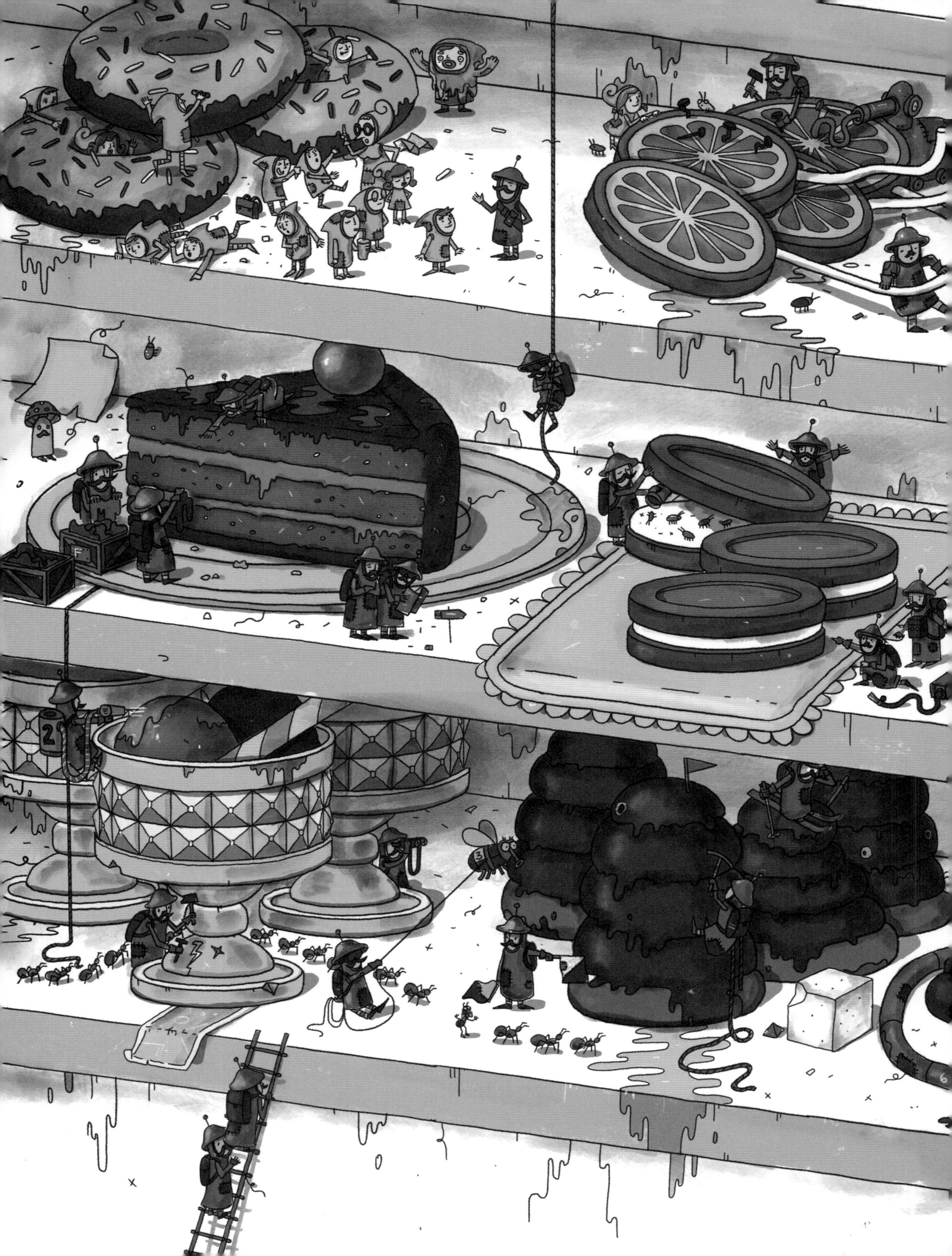
F
2
3

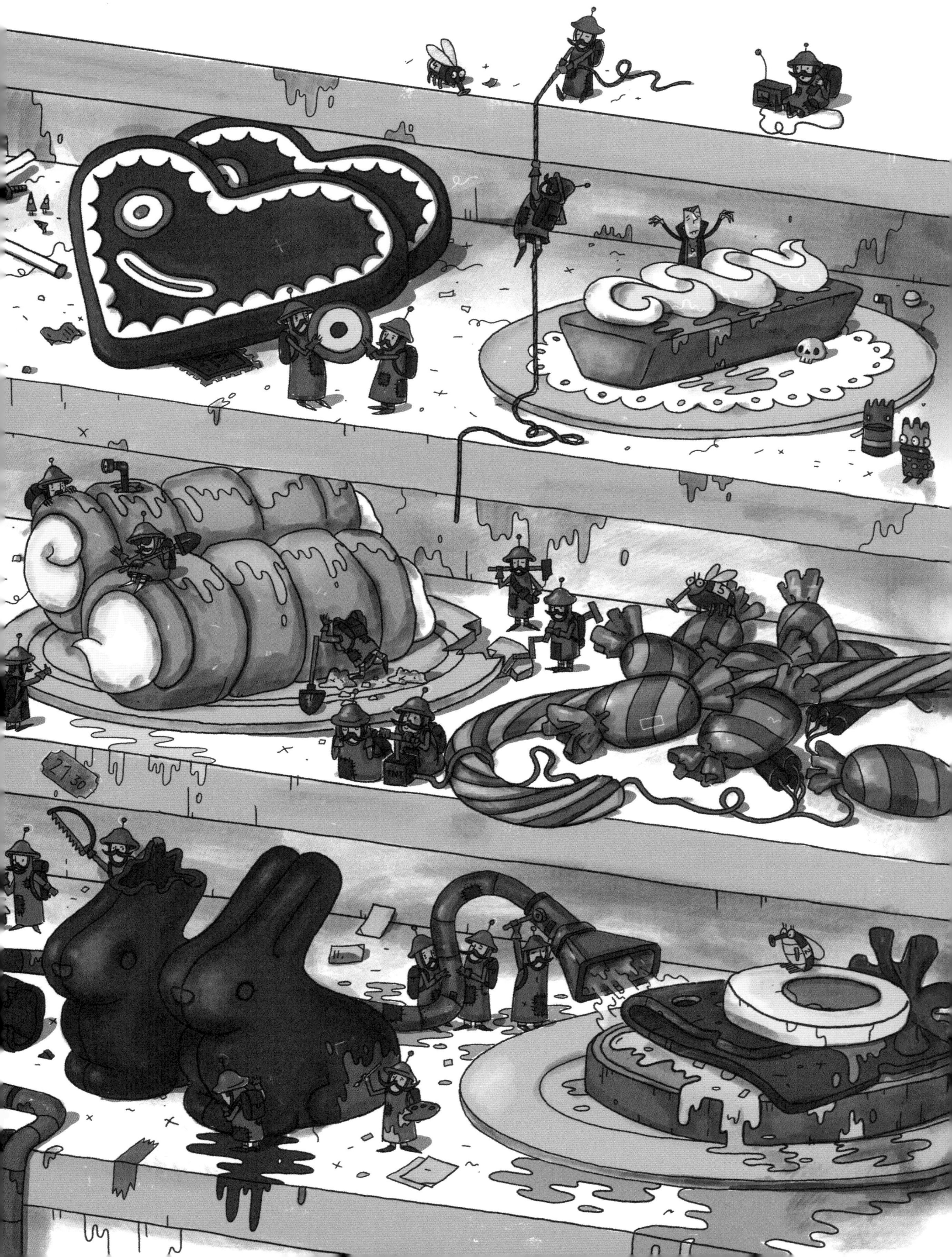
21:30
TNT

Dr Louse the entomologist arrived with a trained fly on a leash. He wasted no time in getting started. “Well, kids,” he said briskly, “yours is the third class I’ve spoken to today, so I’ll keep it brief. Every patisserie worth its salt has a few flies in the ointment. Heh heh. In the insect zoo at this patisserie, we keep specially trained moths, bees, wasps, ants, spiders, cockroaches, earwigs, barklice and silverfish. We even have a few ghost insects and ice crawlers. All of them help us make cakes and sandwiches stale, collapse whipped cream, and turn cream puffs rancid and marble cakes crusty. Last but not least, they come to the aid of our dauber colleagues as they work in the display cases and shop window.”

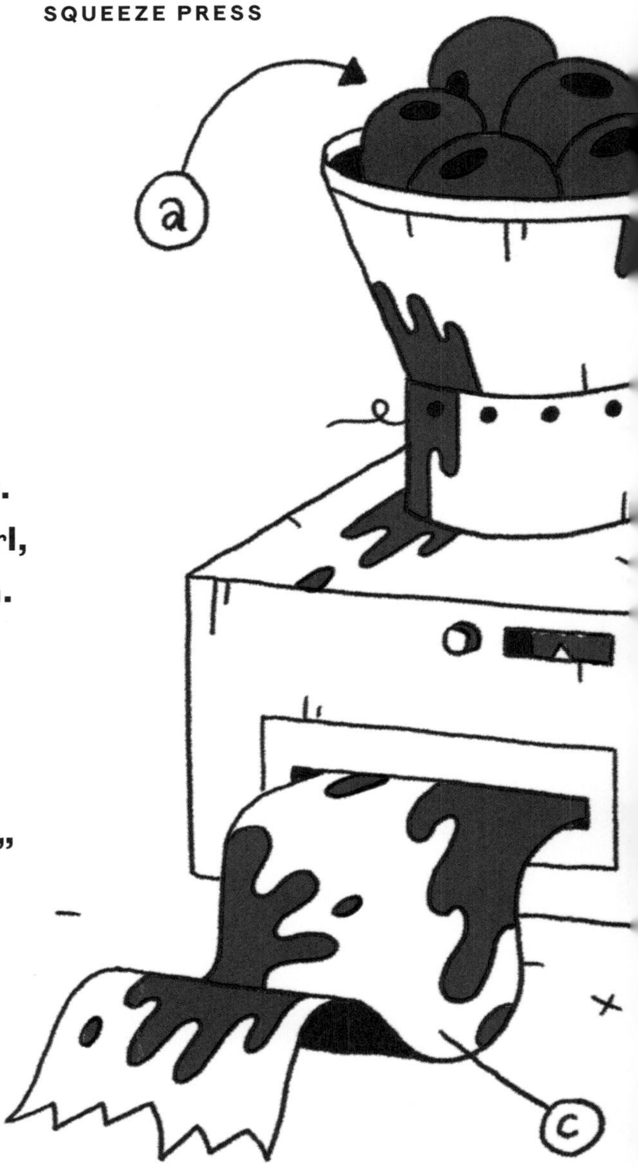
SEMI-AUTOMATIC BILBERRY
SQUEEZE PRESS
a
c

I was already struggling to suppress my yawns. But then my attention was drawn by a little girl, who had just come into the shop with her mom. I say ‘little girl’, but of course for us entropic elves all you humans are absolutely enormous, even the little ones. The mom kept shouting at the girl. “Don’t touch, Margaret! Don’t knock anything over, Margaret! Wait here, Margaret!” I didn't need to be a genius to deduce that the girl’s name was Margaret.

She came really close to the shelf where our class was, so I got a good, close look at her. Although the dress she wore was horribly clean, she’d just got some melted ice cream on it, and her mom was scolding her for this.

I couldn’t understand the logic behind the lecture – the ice cream was the one thing that made the insufferably clean, crisply ironed dress look a bit normal! They brought Margaret a big box, and opened it to show her the contents. It was Margaret’s birthday cake – she was six today. And that's when I had my idea!

"Hey, Skim," I said, turning to my friend. He wasn't paying much attention to Dr Louse's explanation either; greedily, he was eyeing the boxes of cocoa arranged on the shelf immediately above ours. "I'm going to make myself scarce for a while, okay?" I pointed at the open birthday-cake box, which was directly beneath us. When Mrs Frosting had mentioned that someone might carry us off in a box, it had struck me as a good idea to let this happen to me. "I'll get a glimpse of how people live in their homes, and then I'll hurry back to Headquarters. I may as well make good use of the teleport. But Mrs Frosting mustn't find out that I'm missing!"

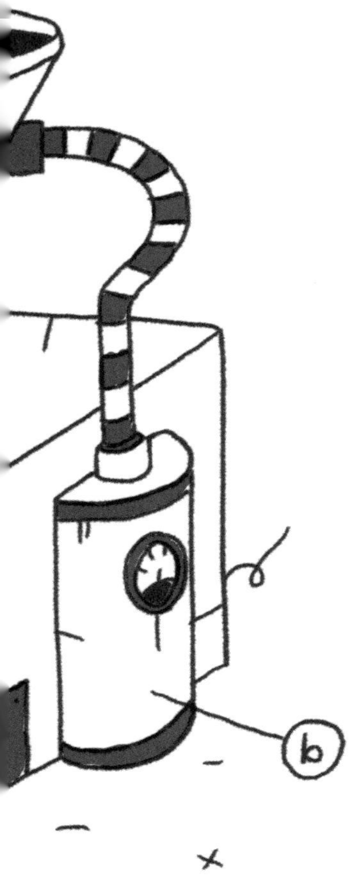
b

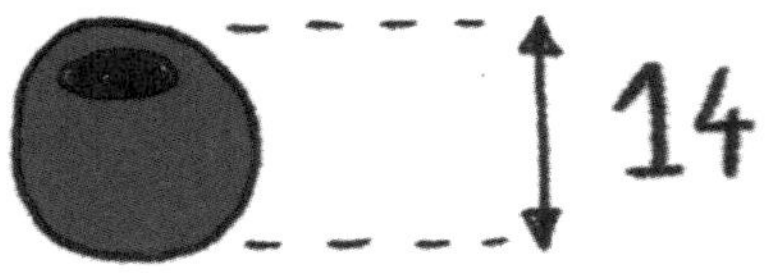
14

"I don't get it," said Skim. He's sometimes a bit slow-witted. Again I pointed to the cake in the box beneath us and explained it all patiently. "I'm going to jump into that cake box and get myself taken to those humans' home. You'll cover for me so that Mrs Frosting doesn't find out I'm gone and call me back like she did with Badegg and Wormold. As soon as I've had a look around, I'll teleport myself back out and no one will be any the wiser. Do you get it now?"

"But why? Won't it be dangerous? What are you going to do there? It seems a bit odd to me..." Skim babbled. But I knew I didn't have much time. "Just stand in front of me so that no one sees me and look as though there's nothing going on. Come on, be a pal!"

I hid behind Skim, who tried to look nonchalant but was obviously nervous; he kept turning to look at me. Fortunately, Mrs Frosting's attention was fully absorbed by the talk on the secret lives of flies, and she didn't notice a thing.

I looked down. The box was quite a long way down, but the cake had lots of whipped cream on it, so my landing should be a fluffy one. There was no time to hesitate. Into the air I leaped.

No sooner had I landed softly in whipped cream, right next to a towering marzipan rose, than the lid of the box closed. The last thing I saw, high above me on the shelf, before everything went dark, was Skim with a look of horror on his face. My face wore a smile. I was on my way to Margaret's home!

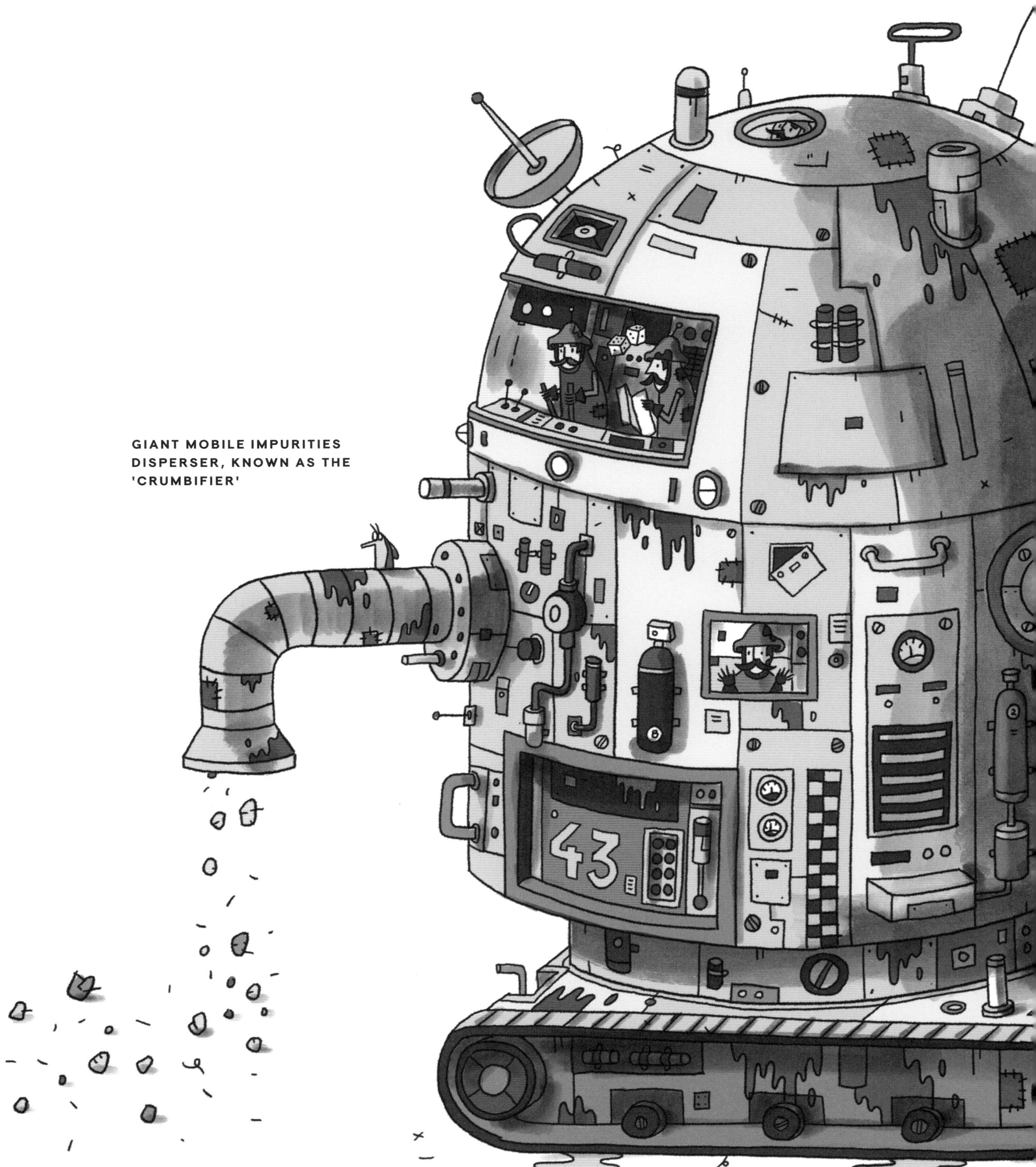
43

GIANT MOBILE IMPURITIES DISPERSER, KNOWN AS THE 'CRUMBIFIER'

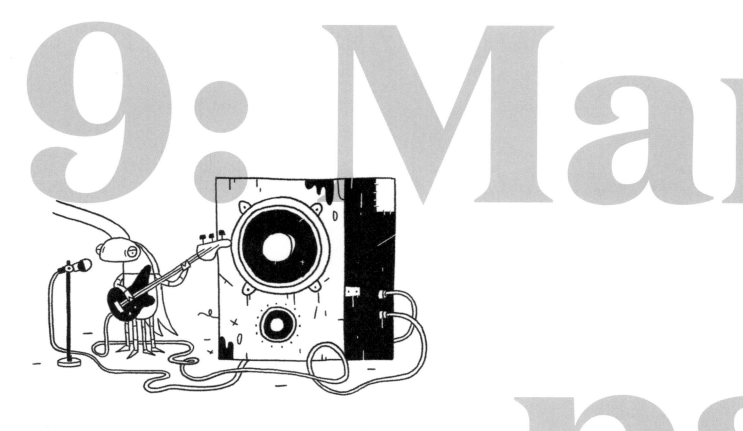

I don't know how many times you've traveled in a box with a cake inside, but for me, this was the very first time. To begin with, I was a bit scared – it was totally dark in there, the box was never still, and all kinds of unknown sounds reached me from the vast human town outside. Regrettably I didn't have much time to listen to these, as a trained cricket soon got to work. Dr Louse the entomologist had just told us that crickets were taken straight from the special incubator they were bred in to cake, sweets and cookie boxes, so that as soon as they reached a human home, they could dash under a cupboard or bed and start up their melodious incessant chirping.

So I listened to the cricket's impressive warm-up routine, admiring how the paratroopers seemed to have thought of everything. Because as I'm sure you know, crickets are omnivores – there was no way that Margaret's cake would arrive at her party untouched and like new. The patisserie paratroopers were way ahead of the game!

Before long, I was even able to peek out of the box: a bit of sunlight got in through holes here and there in the cardboard, applied by the hole-punchers at work. I climbed to the top of the cake and slid about in the cream. This was such fun. I was sorry Skim wasn't here to share it with me. He would have come up with so many creative ways to make the most of that cake!

I decided that I, too, would make an improvement to Margaret's cake, as a way of thanking her for having me to visit. My expertise doesn't stretch to souring cream and spoiling jelly, of course, but there *was* something I could do with the lettering on the top of the cake, which spelled

MARGARET'S name.

Then, at lat, we were "home." I felt the box being set down and then opened. Before I could get my bearings, a woman's voice started yelling. "Help! A beetle! Aagh!" Then all hell broke loose – all the giant humans who had come to Margaret's party started chasing the poor little cricket, meanwhile shouting things like: "It's a cricket! Catch it, or we won't get a wink of sleep tonight!"; "Do something, *Charles!*"; "Quickly, before it gets under the cupboard!" To all appearances, the humans weren't at all pleased to have brought home a cricket. They caught it in the end. To my great relief, they tossed it out of the window without doing it any harm.

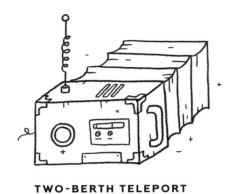

TWO-BERTH TELEPORT
WITH BELLOWS

I was quite shocked by all this. Why should humans be bothered by a cricket? Anyway, I made use of the confusion to scamper out of the box and climb to the top of an enormous fridge, allowing me a fantastic view. And this was some house – I'd never seen anything like it. The floor had been wiped, the carpet had been vacuumed, the walls were an unblemished white, and the cloth on the table didn't have a single hole in it or the tiniest stain. The whole place was unbelievably (and uncomfortably) tidy! On top of that, everything was terrifyingly massive.

Fortunately, I saw where our paratroopers were straight away. Armed with splashers, stainers, hole-punches and greasers, they were scattered about the apartment. Right in front of me was a dust-ball cannon, which was firing bundles of dust down the back of the fridge at regular intervals. I would need to keep myself well hidden – if a paratrooper noticed me, I'd be in big trouble. So I grabbed a medium-sized bundle of dust to use as a disguise.

One amazing thing was, even though the house was filled with paratroopers working tirelessly to age, disintegrate and dirty everything around them, the humans kept sabotaging their work. Margaret's mom was the worst – she was forever rushing around, removing dust, wiping surfaces clean, buffing things up and straightening things out.

THREAD-TEARER

TUG 'N TEAR!

I just couldn't wrap my head around it. Given the chance, my own mom would have exchanged a few cross words with this fussy lady, I can tell you. "What do you think this is, a cleaner's? Spill something on that floor – now! Those spotless plates and cutlery are an absolute disgrace! Put a rip in that disgustingly ironed tablecloth!" My mother knows a thing or two about mess-making.

Definitely the low point was when they noticed
my fine work with the lettering that now spelled

MAGARRET

on the cake. They got terribly angry about
it. Not a single one of them appreciated my
masterly chocolate typo. Margaret herself was
so upset that she burst into tears.

I looked on, stunned. Why didn't Margaret
like my way of thanking her? In the end, they
returned the lettering to its original state. After
that, Margaret blew out her six candles and
began to unwrap her presents. And how awful
these were! A brand-new cuddly teddy bear
with all its fur, a terribly clean, holeless T-shirt
in brilliant colors, and a pristine modern pink
tablet with a completely unscratched screen.
Margaret didn't seem to me to be an especially
naughty child, so why didn't she deserve some
decent old presents? Couldn't they give her at
least a fraying, well-used jumprope? Or a lovely
brown moldy apple? No such luck. I wouldn't
wish such a miserable birthday party on anyone,
not even Badegg or Wormold.

But then the tablet slipped from Margaret's
grasp and fell to the floor. I saw our telescopic
webbifiers run straight over to it and imprint
a really beautiful, twelve-legged crack spider on
the screen. What quick, well-coordinated work
it was! I'd love to be so sure-handed with my
letters.

DUST-BALL CANNON

NEVER MISSES ITS TARGET (BUT IT WOULDN'T BE THE END OF
THE WORLD IF IT DID). BECAUSE OF ITS ABSOLUTE SIMPLICITY,
WORKING THE CANNON IS A RELAXING CHANGE OF PACE FOR
A PARATROOPER. VERY THERAPEUTIC

I waited in suspense for how Margaret and her parents would react to this. Well, what would you expect? Margaret burst into tears again, getting an earful from her dad for her trouble. She couldn't be trusted not to break anything the moment she was given it, he said. Mom picked up the tablet, telling Dad that Margaret was simply too young for it, so there was no need for him to shout at her. Dad complained that his daughter got her clumsiness from her mother. Now Mom was angry, too; Dad should stop trying to blame her for something that wasn't her fault, she said. Dad asked Mom if she knew how much the tablet had cost, because tablets don't grow on trees (that was pretty obvious, I thought). While all this was going on, Margaret cried and pleaded for her present back ...

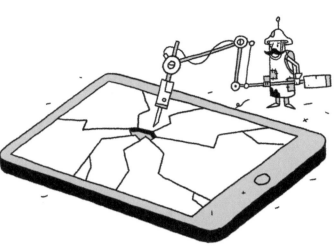

TELESCOPIC WEBBIFIER

"GLASSCRACK!": THE WEBBIFIER UNITS'
CELEBRATORY CRY

That was when it dawned on me. It came as such a shock that at first I didn't want to admit that it might be true. But the longer I watched the troubled birthday celebrations unfold below me, the more convinced of this truth I became: humans didn't like entropic elves at all.

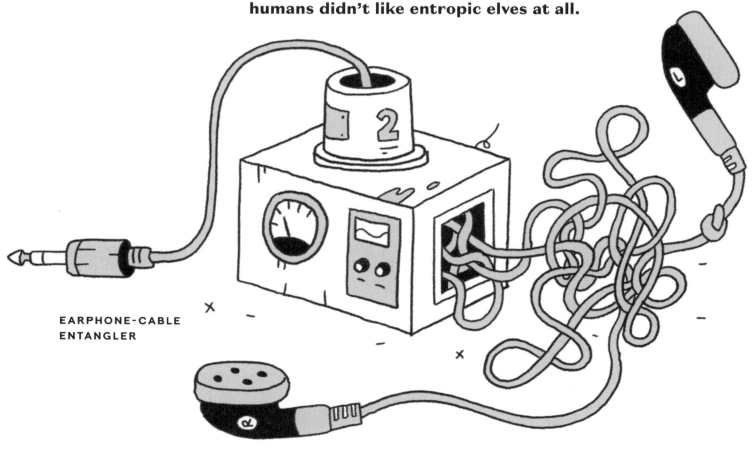

**EARPHONE-CABLE
ENTANGLER**

What a dreadful discovery this was! I'd been looking forward to getting to know the human world since I was born. I'd been working really hard at jumbling words and even whole sentences, and I'd always been impatient to strike out on my own as a paratrooper. Now I learned that no one in the human world appreciated my work. I realized that humans liked things that were nice, clean, neat and new, not old, soiled, jumbled-up or falling apart. So what was the point of Professor Block's classes? Why did my dad keep telling me my work created such important bother in the human world? Bother was unappreciated! At the Crystal Zilch Awards, when Uncle Remoudou urged us to work tirelessly to make the world a better place, what could he have meant? We didn't make the world a better place for humans – we made it worse!

In my agitation, I became careless. I was surprised by an elderly paratrooper, who'd spotted me behind my bundle of dust. "Well, well, well. What have we here, then? A lost pupil from a school trip, perhaps?" he snapped at me, making me terribly afraid. "Where are your classmates? Where's the supervising teacher?" His moustache crackled with menace. "There's nothing at all for you here, so why are you hiding? What have you been up to? I must report you to Headquarters immediately!"

All the anger and disappointment I felt from what I'd just seen, rose up in me. I pointed at Margaret and her parents and yelled at him. "I haven't been *up* to anything. But I've seen what you do, and it harms and hurts people!" The paratrooper was quite taken aback. "We entropic elves do nothing but make humans upset," I went on. "What is all our work good for?"

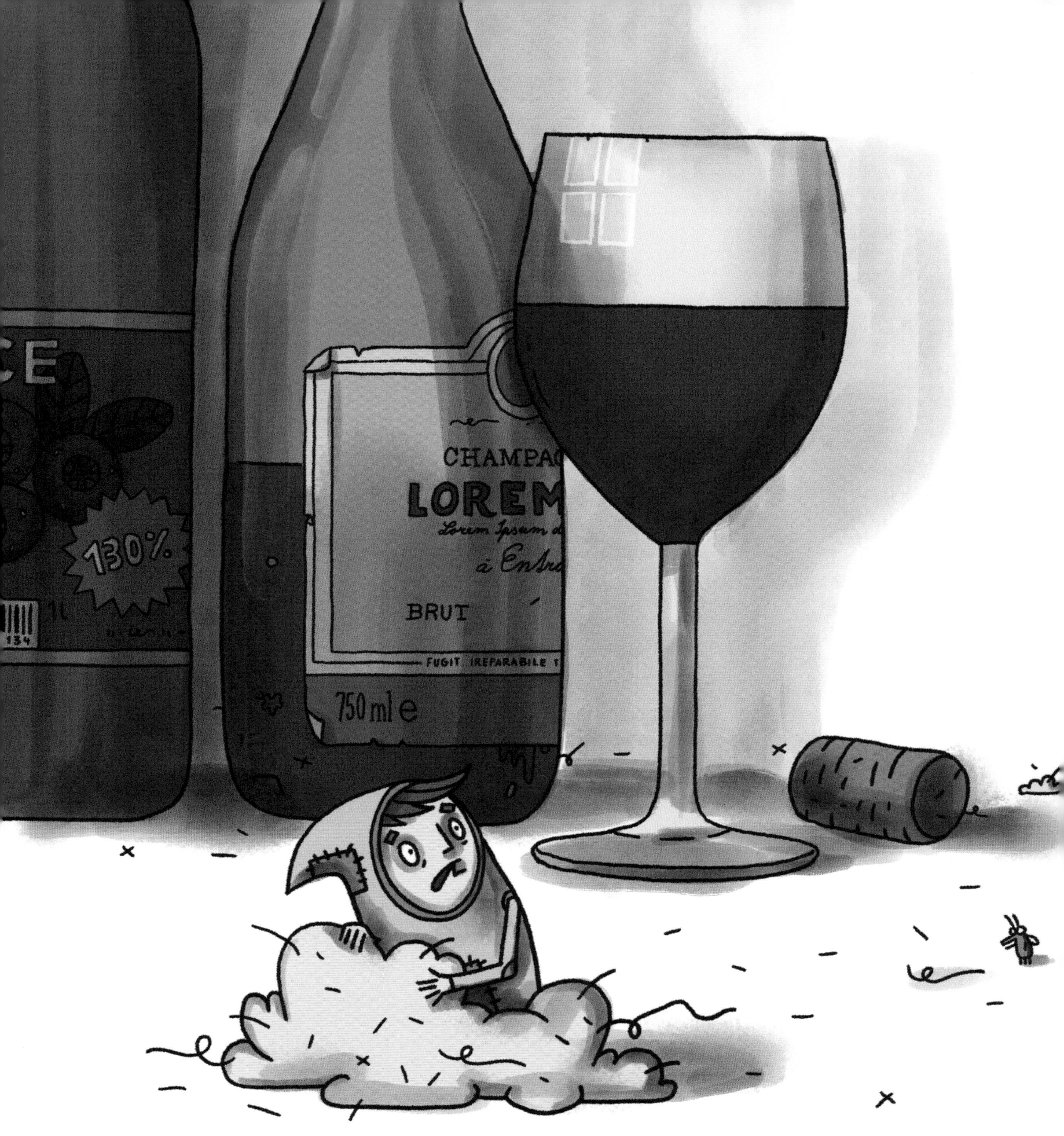
CE
130%
1L
134
CHAMPAG
LOREM
Lorem Ipsum d
à Entra
BRUT
FUGIT IREPARABILE T
750 ml e

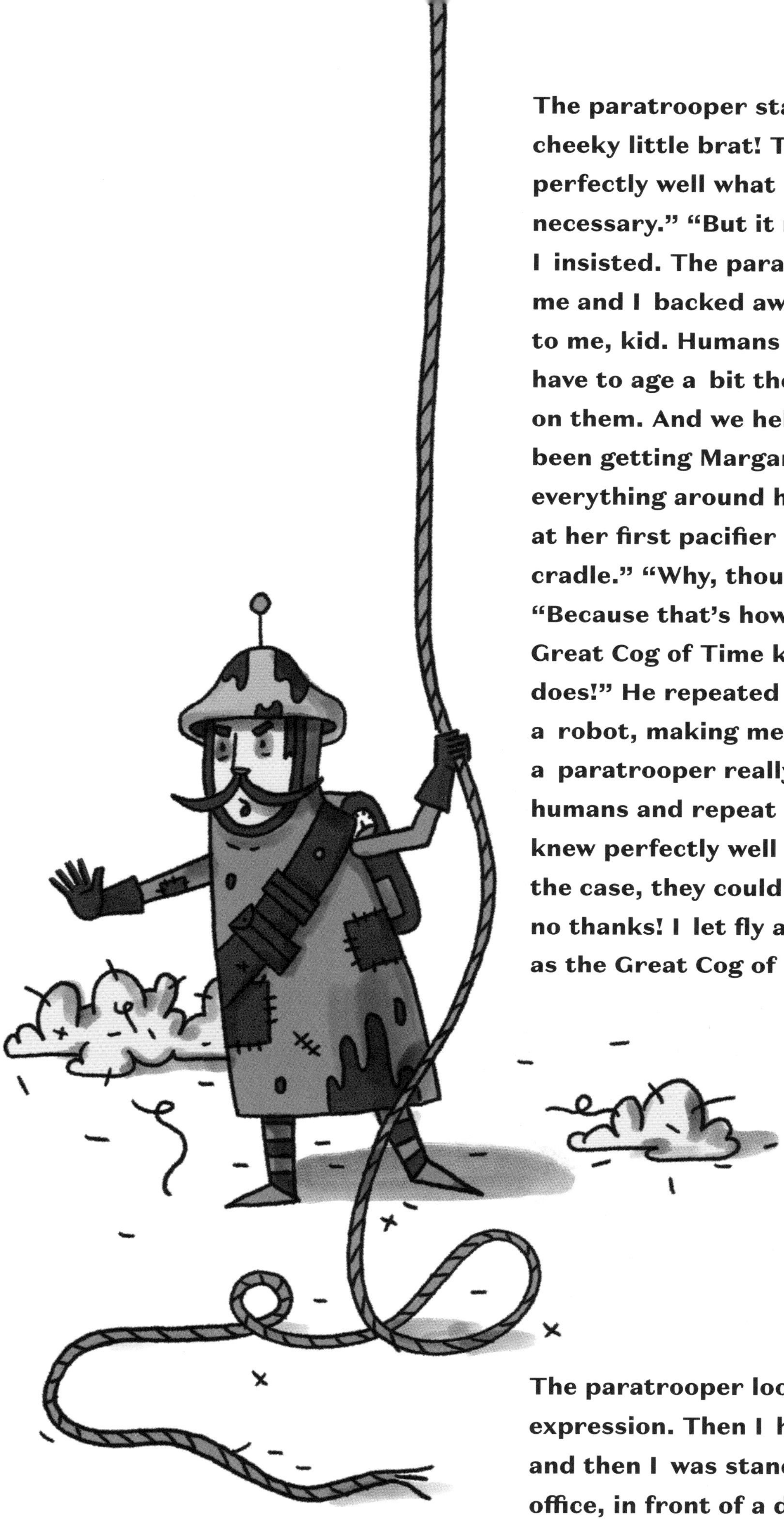

The paratrooper stared at me wild-eyed. "You cheeky little brat! The Great Cog of Time knows perfectly well what it does and why aging is so necessary." "But it makes everyone unhappy!" I insisted. The paratrooper took a step towards me and I backed away instinctively. "Now listen to me, kid. Humans don't get it at first. They have to age a bit themselves before it dawns on them. And we help them get there. I've been getting Margaret used to the notion that everything around her ages since I scraped away at her first pacifier when she was still in her cradle." "Why, though?" I was still shouting. "Because that's how it has to be, and the Great Cog of Time knows perfectly well what it does!" He repeated these words of wisdom like a robot, making me more disappointed still. Did a paratrooper really just play spiteful tricks on humans and repeat that the Great Cog of Time knew perfectly well what it did? Well, if that was the case, they could count me out. Thanks, but no thanks! I let fly at him: "There's no such thing as the Great Cog of Time. It's just made up!"

The paratrooper looked at me with a grim expression. Then I heard the farting sound, and then I was standing in the headmaster's office, in front of a displeased Professor Block and a stern Mrs Frosting who held the big walkie-talkie that operated the teleports.

10: Cri
punish

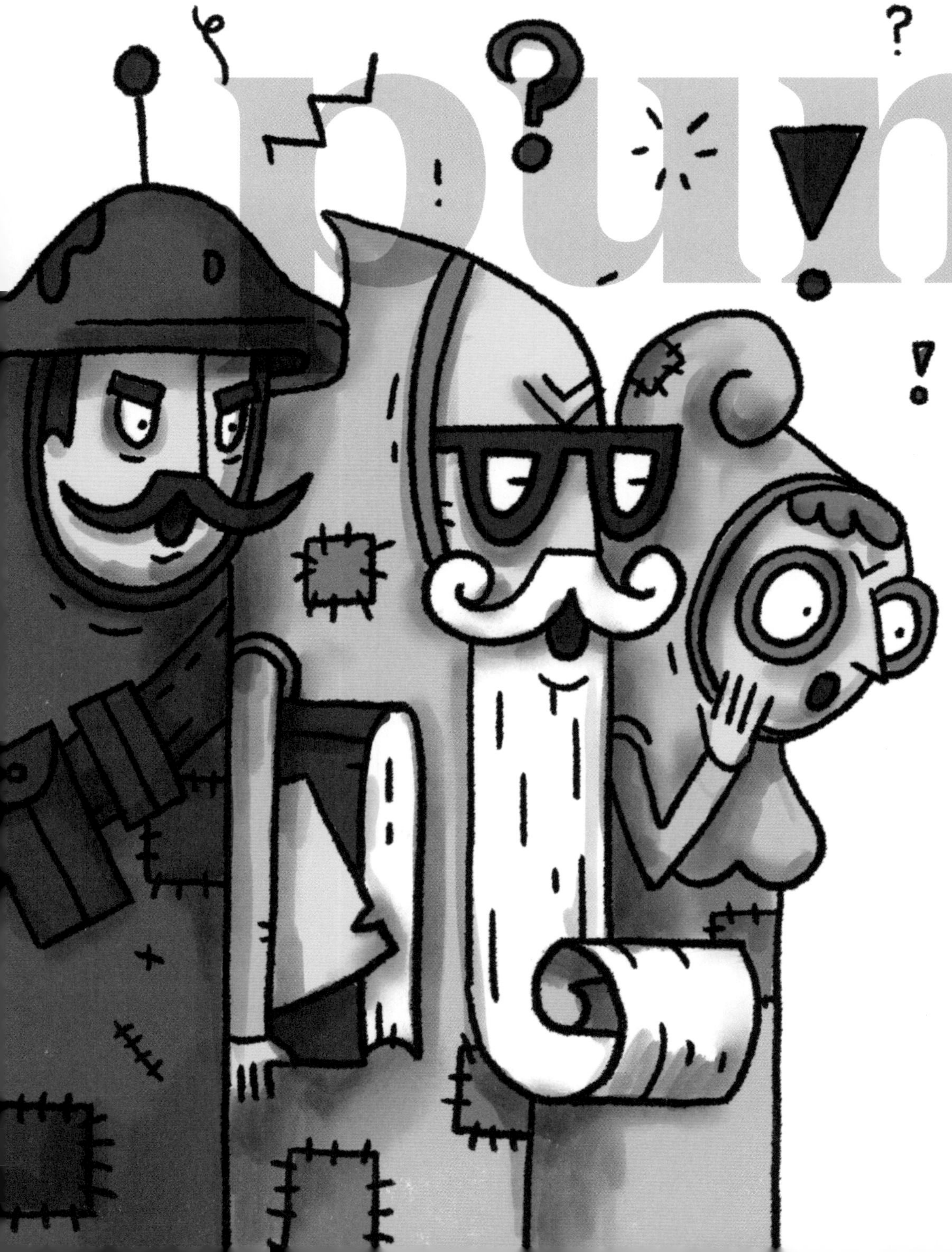

me and
nment

Man, was I ever in trouble! Professor Block and Mrs Frosting weren't the only teachers in the principal's office, either. About half of the teaching staff were there, as well as Broom the caretaker. But the biggest surprise was to find Skim there, crouching in the corner, looking guilty. The very same Skim I'd asked to cover for me so no one would find out about my little excursion. This was too much for me to take. I was steaming! Best friends are supposed to keep their promises. If they don't, then they're not best friends.

"Pupil Tyro!" boomed Block. "Typo," Frosting corrected him. "Typo," Block corrected himself. "Not only have you acted in violation of school rules, you have violated the fundamental rule that binds all entropic elves! You have entered the human world without supervision, notwithstanding the fact that you are but a second-grade PSAT pupil." "Third," Frosting corrected him. "Third," Block corrected himself irritably. "What do you have to say in your defense, before I expel you from this school?" Still upset by what I'd seen in the house of Margaret's family, I looked Block in the eye and said, "Expel me if you wish. I couldn't care less. I don't want to spoil humans' lives anymore!"

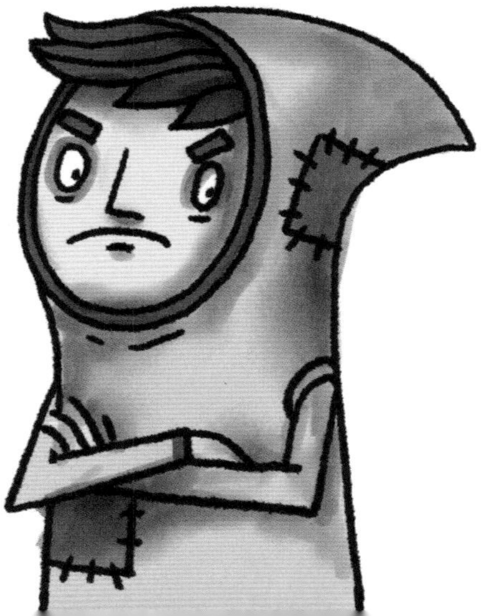

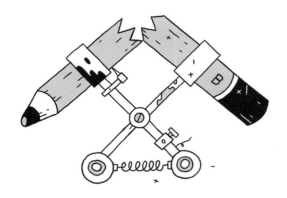

SPRUNG PENCIL-BREAKER
(B HARDNESS)

After I had spoken, a surprised silence fell on the room. I heard a slow drip coming from Skim. "What on earth are you saying, Typie?" asked Mrs Frosting. She looked stunned. Still furious, I explained. "I saw little Margaret burst into tears each time our paratroopers broke something. They didn't make her happy at all – no, quite the opposite. And her parents got into an argument about it. Plus, nobody appreciated the ingenious typo I made on the cake! So what I want to know is, why do you teach us all this stuff when it causes nothing but anguish in the human world?"

The teachers exchanged looks of bewilderment, Skim gaped at me and Professor Block scratched his chin. "Let me tell you, young elf, that the Great Cog of Time knows perfectly well what it does and why aging is so important!" he said. "I've heard that before. The Great Cog of Time is a great load of nonsense!" I replied.

That just about settled it. Although in the end they didn't expel me, they kept me in the headmaster's office for an hour of reprimands and instruction. That traitor Skim kept gesturing for my attention the whole time, but it was my intention never to speak to him again. Headmaster Block finally came up with the following plan: "The pupil Tyro will be sent to a mildew cultivating farm, where he will work as a mothherd. There he will learn the meaning of the word 'discipline'." Having corrected 'Tyro' to 'Typo', Frosting called my parents to give them the news.

On hearing that I'd run off to the human world without permission, my mom almost passed out. My dad was livid with me and accepted Block's punishment without a word. On that farm I'd get a taste of real work and stop fooling around with things I didn't understand, he told me.

I felt a bit sorry for my mom, even though I was mad as heck with everyone; Skim for having betrayed me, Block for making me work as a mothherd, my parents for their failure to tell me the truth about the human world, plus the whole world and every entropic elf in it. I never wanted to make another typo or see another teacher. I thought all paratroopers were embarrassing. That aging was hateful. All I could think of was making everything stop, once and for all – for the sake of Margaret and all other humans. For my own sake, too. I would find the Great Cog of Time and destroy it. Or else I would prove that there was no such thing and that our work was absolutely pointless. Boy, would I show them all!

But the moths were a bit of a problem. You may imagine working on a farm to be a fun experience. Or you may imagine it as a real yawn. Neither is true. Carpet moths are the most stubborn creatures I know; when they make up their mind for or against something, not even a herd of mites can move them. So keeping them in one place and making sure they grazed only where they were supposed to, was a real chore. And no sooner had the moths been delivered to human gardens and greenhouses than caterpillars of the common clothes moth were entrusted to my care. These are so greedy that I could barely keep the wardrobe stocked. They would get through a whole coat in half a day, and you can surely imagine what a struggle it was for me to drag coat after coat to the farm, even with two teams of snails at my disposal. By the time all the clothes moths had been delivered to human homes, the next generation of carpet moths was hatching.

And so it went, over and over again. It was a dreadful slog, and never a moment's rest.

BUCKET OF STAINS

CORNER GRUBBER

A MEMBER OF THE VANDALIBRIS FAMILY, TOGETHER WITH THE BOOKWORM THE CORNER GRUBBER IS THE BEST-KNOWN BIBLIODEFACER. GRUB GRUB!

67

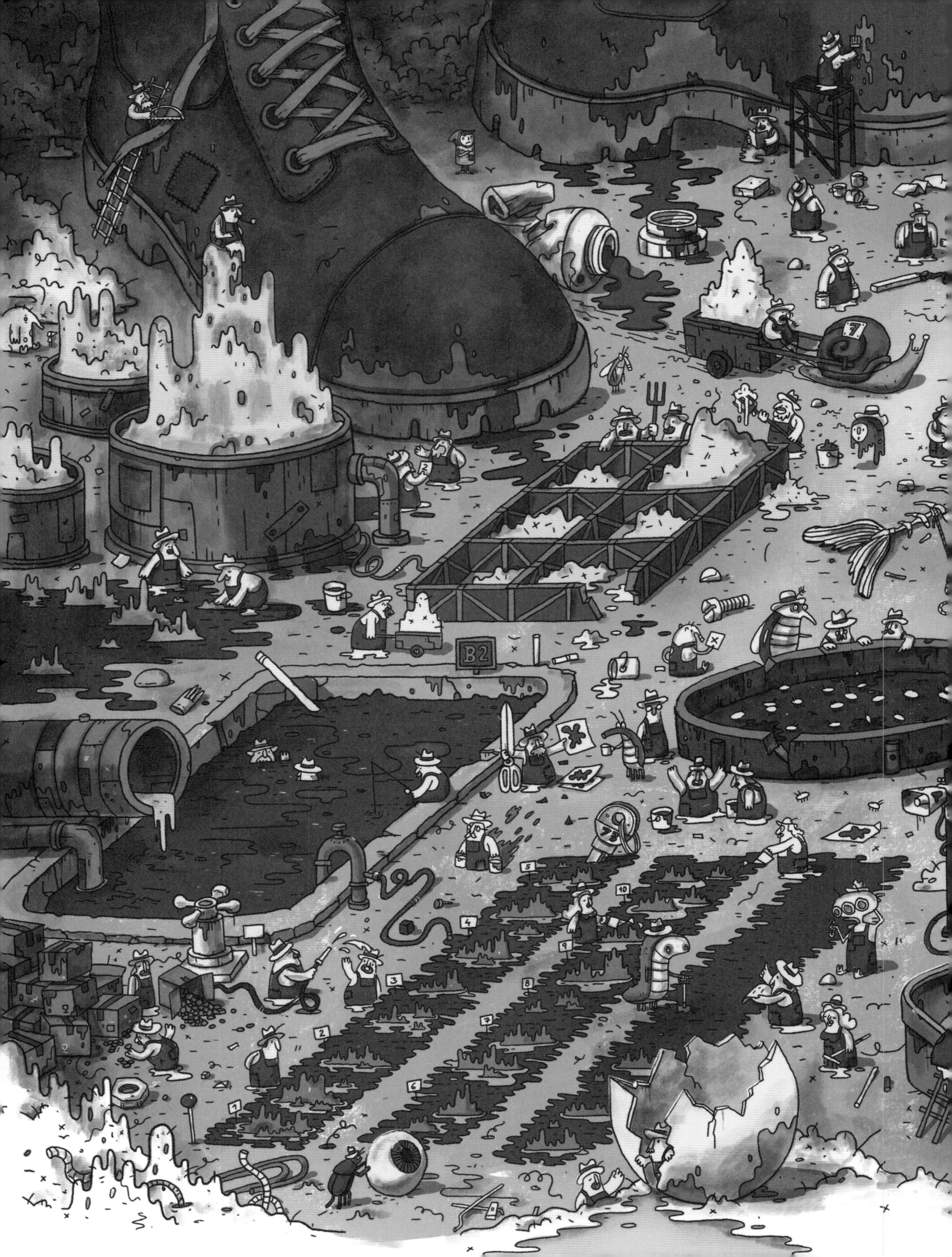
B2

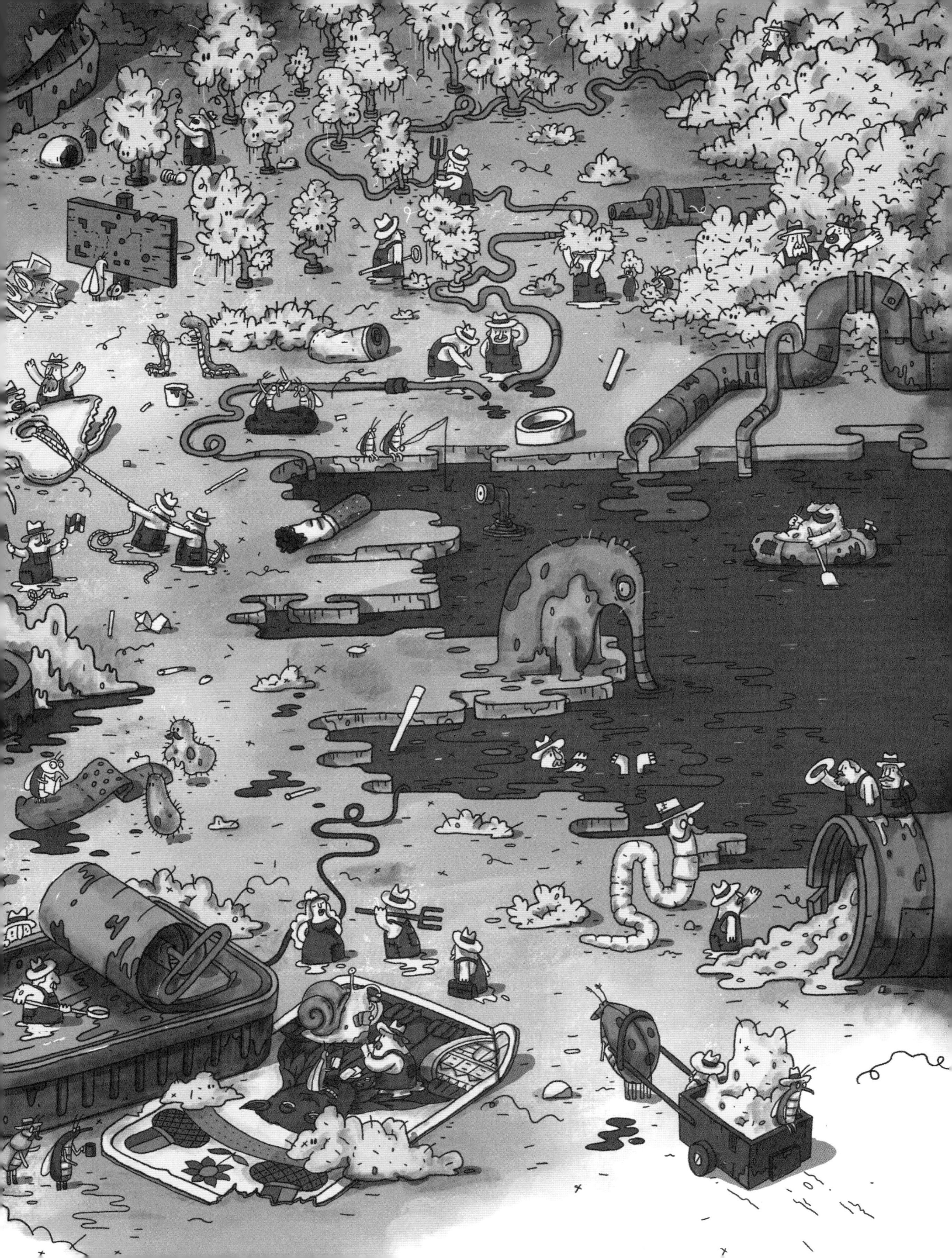

Skim visited me a few times to offer his help, which I ever so curtly declined. I was still so furious that I couldn't speak with him. I didn't believe his claim that he'd told Frosting about what I was doing only out of worry for me. As far as I was concerned, he was a nasty, cocoa-dusted snitch, and I didn't have a single word for him.

So after a while he stopped coming to see me and I was left at the farm all alone. As I did, all the farmers spent the whole day in constant, laborious motion, so there was no time for chit-chat or fun of any kind. Thoughts of the Cog of Time were never far from my mind, although I didn't have the foggiest idea where I should start to look for it.

Remarkably enough, the only entropic elf with whom I occasionally exchanged a few words was Skim's uncle Remoudou. Every day, he and Maurice delivered peelings from the dump, and he always asked me if I would keep an eye on his cart while he conducted the formalities of registering and verifying the quality of his peelings. I always agreed; if you're minding a hundred grazing carpet moths, keeping an eye on a cart or two as well is no problem. Remoudou would return the favor by bringing carpets, coats and sweaters from the dump for the moths. And so we sort of became friends.

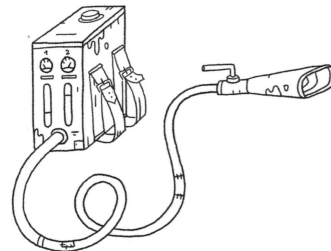

DUST SPRINKLER
(PORTABLE FIELD VERSION)

I discovered that Maurice was surprisingly clever for a dung beetle. When he was in a good mood, he was pretty good at helping me chase after moths. I paid him back by smuggling dog poop from the pavement-pollution stores, which pleased him so much. He happily rolled it into dung balls immediately.

**PRODUCTS AVAILABLE AT
THE PAVEMENT-POLLUTION
STORES**

A ALPINE DUNG (HILL)

B AERODYNAMIC DUNG (AERO)

C CUBOID DUNG (SUGARLUMP)

D FLAME DUNG (CREAMER)

E RUMB DUNG (POOP)

F MAXIMUS SUPERBUS DUNG (STINKER)

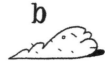

Once, when I was having a rare breather (the
moth caterpillars had just started feasting
on a thick woolen sweater), I asked Uncle
Remoudou about Maurice. Was what they said
true – that he had won him in a game of cards?

"Ahem, of course it's true, Typo," said Remoudou, scratching
the mold behind his ear. "We were playing poker at the dump,
as we always do, when an odd-looking elf joined us at the
table. He didn't look like an entropic – he was a head shorter
than the rest of us, ahem, with a big nose and a yellowish
complexion. I'd never seen him before, and I haven't seen
him since. He said he'd been blown here by the *simoom* –
that's a sand-laden wind from the deserts of Egypt – and was
waiting for the wind to turn around; he wanted to relieve the
boredom of his wait by playing cards with us.

"He was a pretty good gambler, though no
match for old Remoudou, of course. I took
him for everything he had, including our friend
Maurice here. When he first offered Maurice
to me, I wouldn't hear a word of it. Dung
beetles aren't currency, I said. But the next
thing I knew, the wind had got up and the elf
was gone, leaving Maurice here with me. I've
no regrets, though. No regrets at all. He's the
cleverest beetle in the world, and we have lots of
fun together. Don't we, Maurice?"

Remoudou patted Maurice on his wing cases, and Maurice pricked up his antennae. Skim's uncle leaned towards me and said in a half-whisper, "Ahem, in Egypt, you know, dung beetles are called scarabs, and they're sacred." "Sacred?" I didn't understand. "For Egyptians, scarabs are a symbol of eternal life. Some desert elves believe that the Cog of Time has no power over scarabs. Ahem, after they die, it's said that they can choose to be reborn. That may or not be true. What's important to me is that Maurice is my friend and, ahem, together we're going to be dung run champions again. Aren't we, Maurice?"

It was time for Uncle Remoudou and Maurice to leave, and leave they did. I could have sworn that when Remoudou mentioned the Cog of Time, for a brief moment Maurice lost interest in his ball, turned his antennae towards us and winked at me! Although it was the subtlest of winks, I knew full well what it meant. If anyone could take me to the Cog of Time, then that someone was Maurice the dung beetle!

"THIS SEASON, DEVOUR NOTHING BUT RETRO!"

SAYS JAMES KNIT-ONE-PURL-ONE, DIETICIAN FOR CLOTHES-MOTH CATERPILLARS.

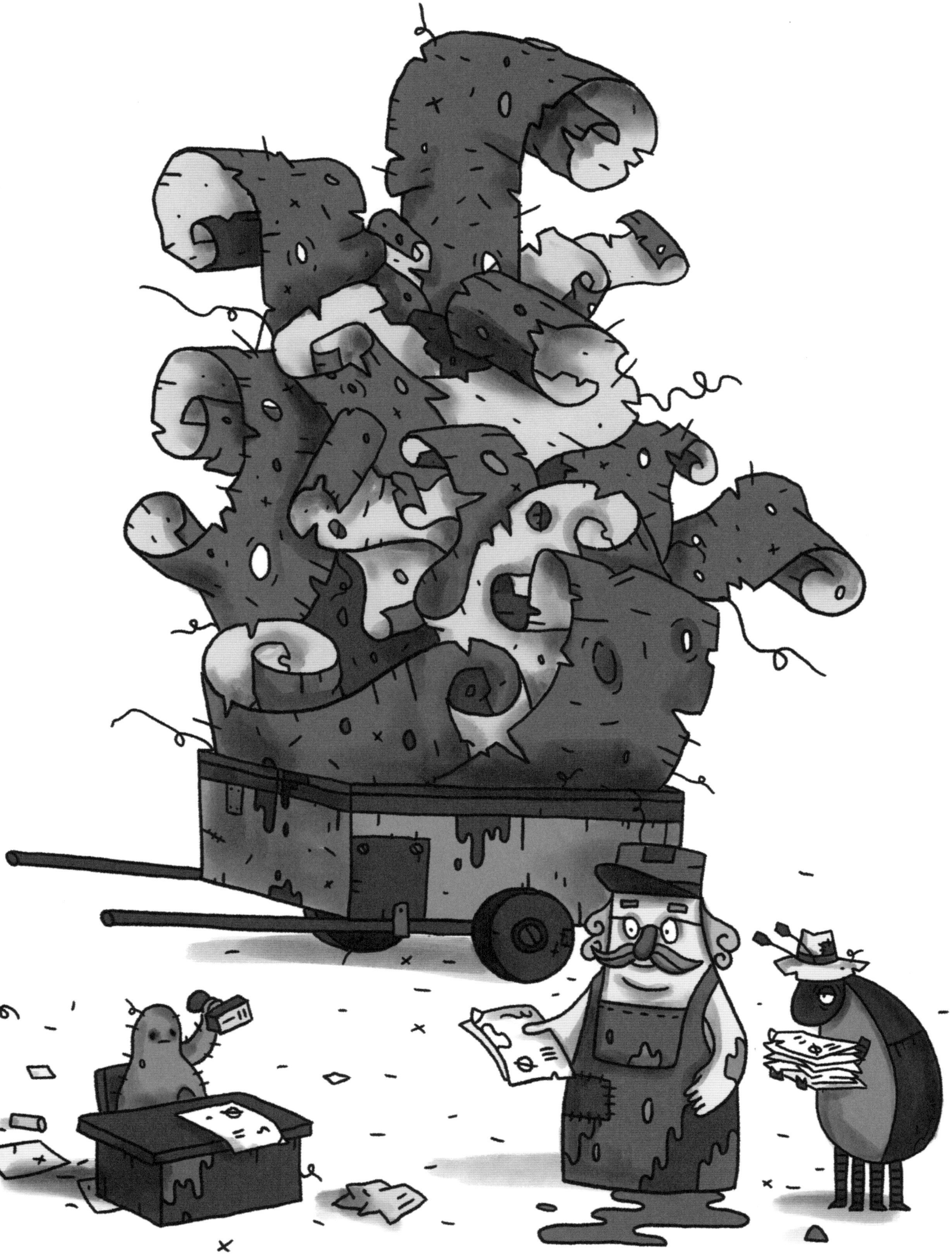

11: D

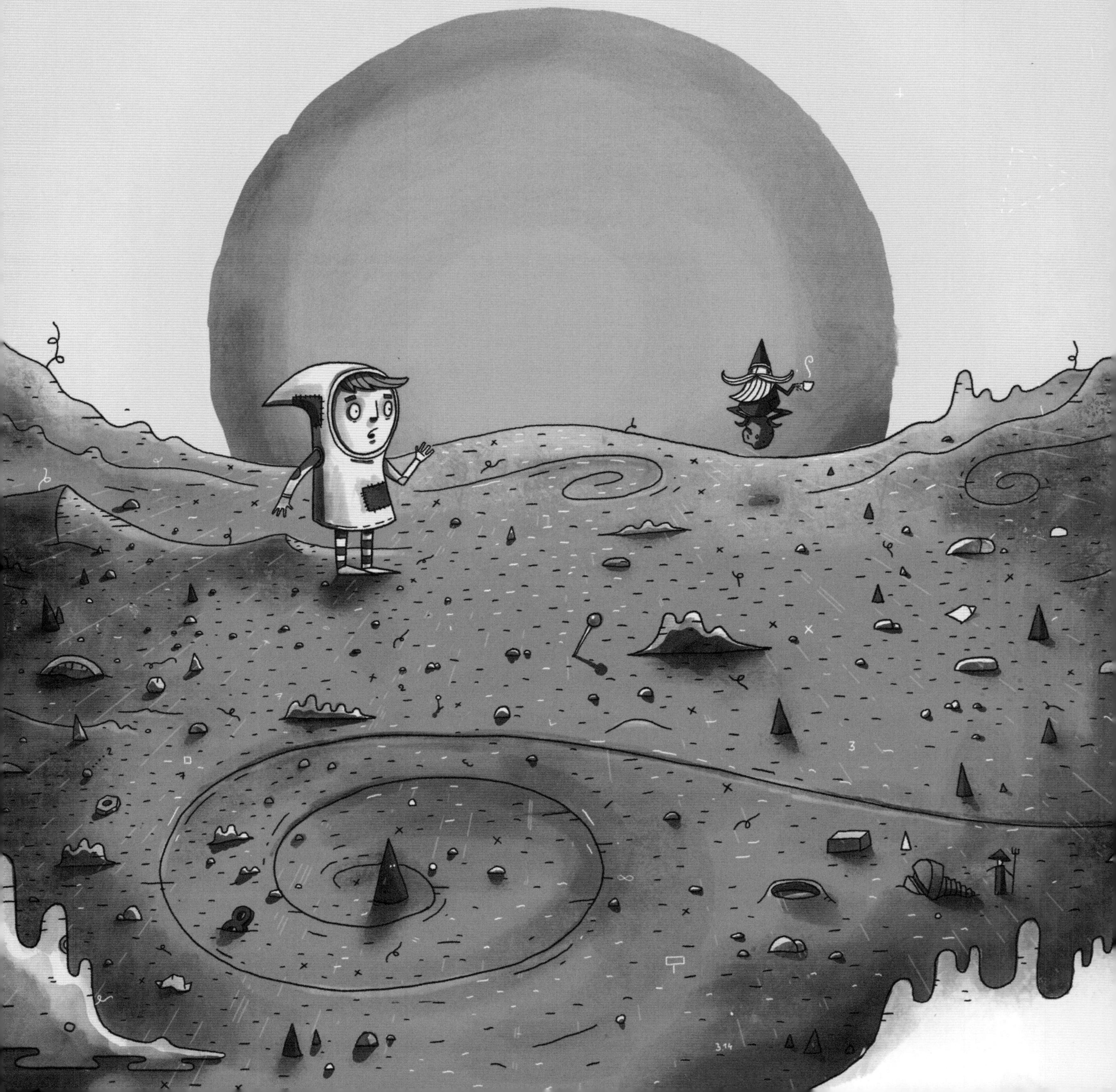

I confess. I hatched a dark plan. I decided to steal Maurice from Uncle Remoudou. I know that stealing is wrong. I was really sorry to have to do it, believe me. But first of all, I was absolutely sure that if Remoudou knew what I was planning, he would never lend me Maurice; secondly, I would give Maurice back as soon as I had destroyed the Cog of Time. Seriously – as soon as all aging was in the past, I would hand Maurice over. Having convinced myself of the justice of my mission, I went straight into action.

When Remoudou and Maurice next came to the farm with their peelings, and Remoudou went off to register, I went over to Maurice and said, "Listen carefully, Maurice. I know that you can understand me. I saw your surprise when I was talking about the Cog of Time. So if you've any idea where it can be found, I'd like you to take me there now, please."

But Maurice didn't move a muscle, except to keep rolling his ball back and forth. And that day he didn't even help me with the carpet moths. Had I upset or offended him somehow? The next day I tried a different approach: I brought him some really good specimens from the dog-poop stores. "I really need to know why aging is so important," I told him. "No one but the Cog of Time can answer that question for me, and no one but you can take me to it. Would you do that for me, Maurice, my good friend?" Maurice took the gift from me, but that was all he did. Although I was disappointed, I decided I would try once more; this time I loaded a cart with as much material from the stores as it would take. As he was pouncing on the poop and slapping it into giant balls, I said, "Come on, Maurice. You know what I want from you. Be a pal – pleease!"

For a moment it seemed that Maurice wasn't going to
do anything even now, and I would have to accept that he
would never help me find the way to the Cog of Time. But
then he leaned on his ball, turned to face me, pricked up his
antennae and winked. I realized that he was getting ready
to leave, and that I should follow him. My heart started
racing – Maurice was going to lead me to the Cog of Time
after all! I would discover the cause of all aging at last, and
maybe I would succeed in stopping it forever! Maurice had
gathered his legs and was trotting away.

And what a pace he traveled at! That dung beetle was
a worthy three-time champion, and it was quite a job for
me to keep up with him. I called after him as I struggled for
breath. "Hey, Maurice! Lemme catch up!" But Maurice kept
up a blistering pace, as if there was a race to be won and,
to win it, he needed to overtake everyone and everything in
the world, perhaps even Time itself.

As I ran behind him with my eyes fixed on his
rapidly rotating ball, I had the impression that
the world was beginning to spin and blur, and that
strange shapes and colors were appearing in it.
By now, the mildew cultivating farm was a long
way behind us. How glad I was that from now on
someone else would have to sweat over those half-
witted moths!

The further away we got, the greater my sense of freedom. It
was no longer a problem for me to run at the same speed as
Maurice; in fact, the very act of running gave me great relief and
joy. Wind rushed by us. On the air I smelled the fragrances of
flowers, trees and exotic fruits as well as the pleasant stenches
of moulds and fungi. The cloying sweetish smell of the forest
gave way to the dust of the road; at one moment I even got
a salty, fishy gust from the sea. Were we running, or was the
whole world spinning under our feet? I whooped and skipped
with delight. "Faster, Maurice! Faster still!! Please!!!"

Then Maurice began to slow down, until he came to a complete stop. When I got my breath back, I saw that we were in the middle of a vast desert. The sun was now scorching. Sand dunes stretched away in every direction I looked.

It occurred to me that maybe Maurice had taken me back to his birthplace in Egypt. "Where've you brought us, Maurice? Feeling homesick?" I asked. When I turned to him, I saw that he was leaning on his ball, apparently asleep.

"Your scarab is tired, it seems," said a strange shriek of a voice from I knew not where. I looked around, but I didn't see anyone. Sand was swirling all about, and hot air above that. The voice shrieked again. "There's no hurry. When they are calm, your eyes will find me."

Then I saw him – an elf small of stature but large of nose. I hadn't noticed him at first because he was as yellow as the sand all around us, the spitting image of the elf in Remoudou's story. He was sitting not far from me. Oddly, it seemed to me that he was sitting not on the sand but slightly above it, hovering in the hot, rippling air. Only once I got closer did I see that he was, in fact, balancing on a grain of sand. Although his eyes were closed against the intense sunlight, I had the sense that they were fixed on me.

CROSS-SECTION OF DUNG BEETLE'S BALL

A CRUST

B MANTLE

C OUTER CORE

D ESSENCE OF THE MATTER

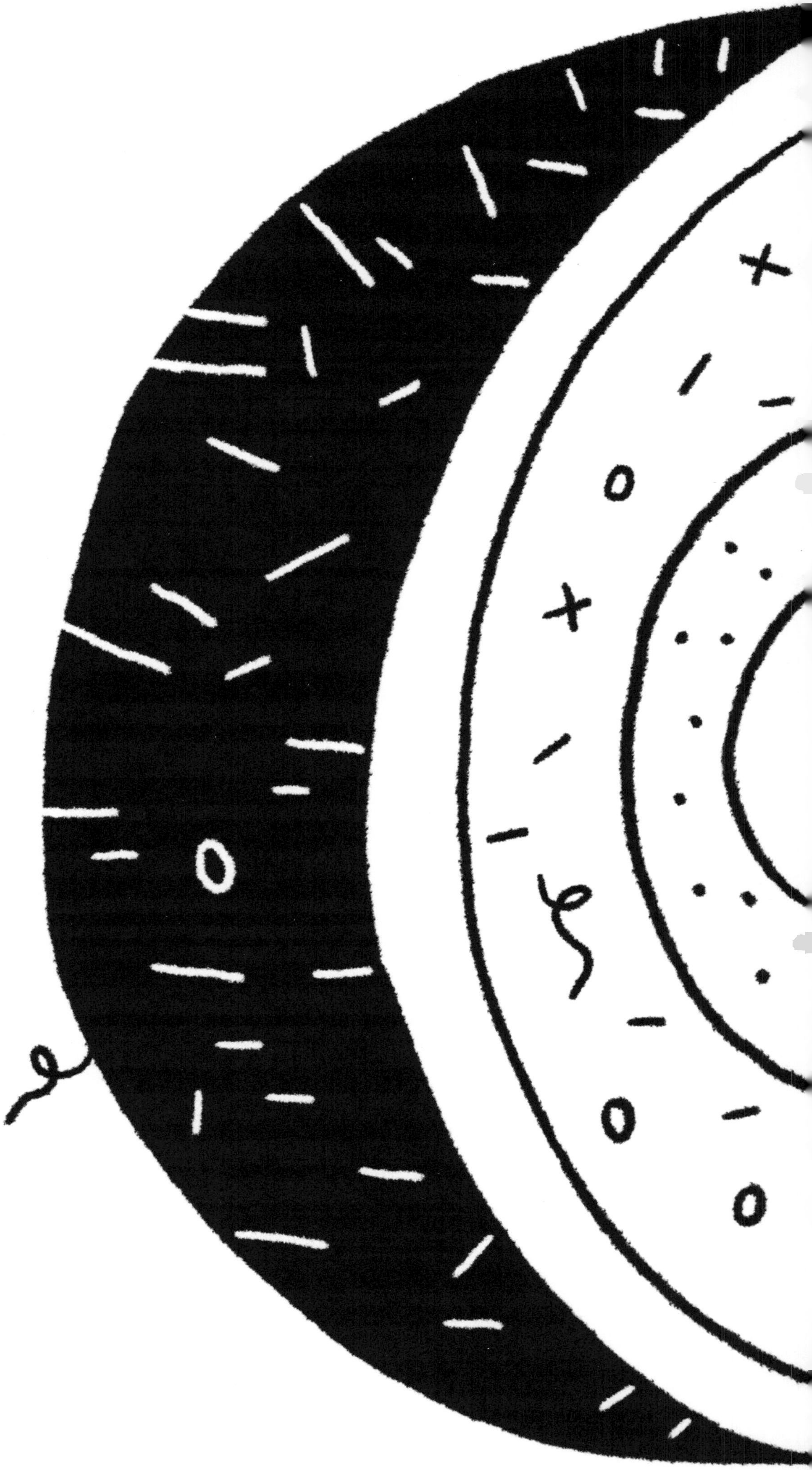

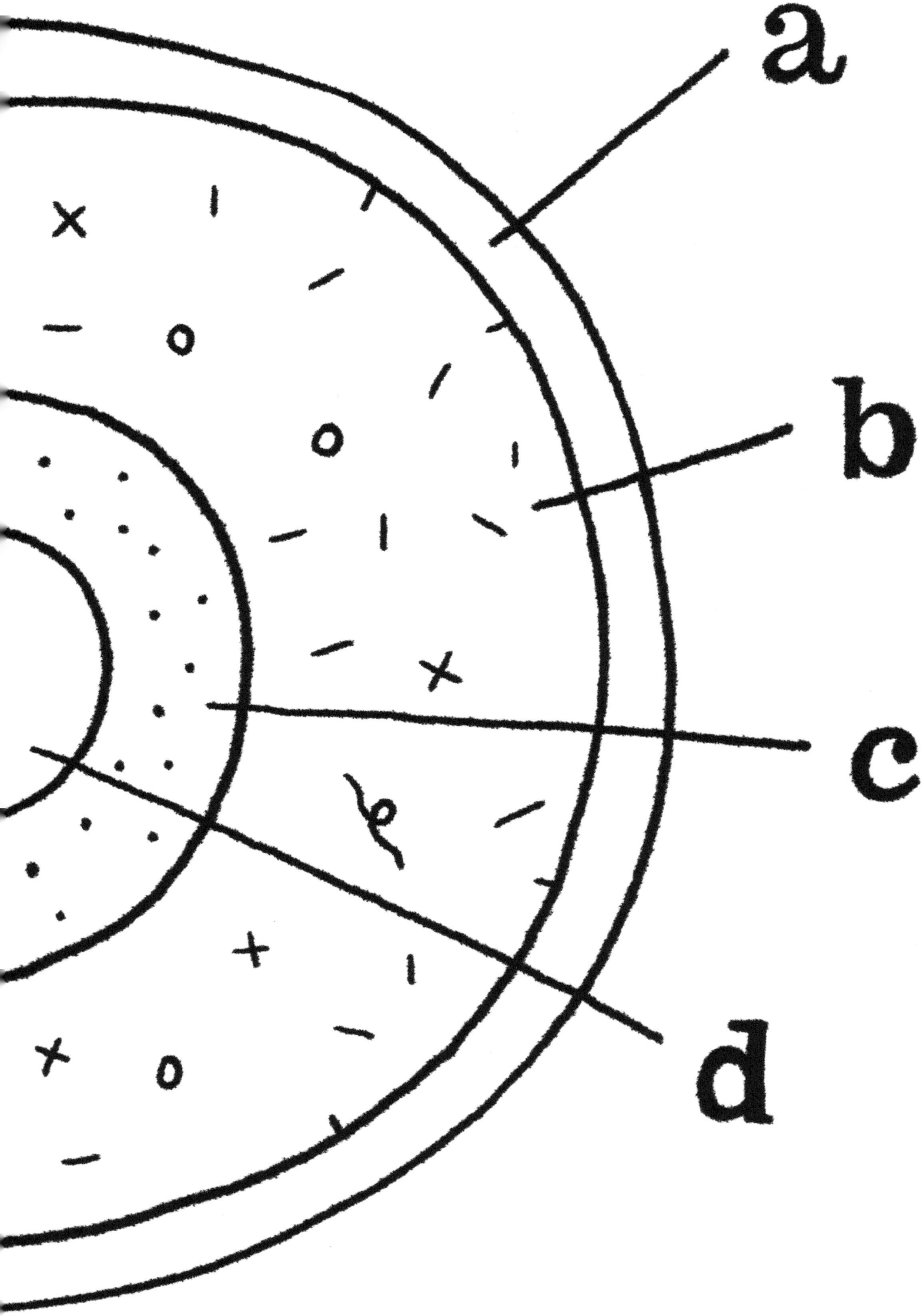
a
b
c
d

"Hello, sir," I began, remembering my manners. "My name's Typo and my dung beetle is called Maurice." The elf half-opened one eye, then closed it again. I didn't know what to do. "We're looking for the Great Cog of Time," I said nervously. "I don't suppose you know where we could find it? If it exists, of course..." Again the elf half-opened one eye; then he opened both eyes and smiled. "The Great Cog of Time? Then you've come to the right place! It is said that whoever counts every grain of sand in the desert will succeed in finding it." I looked about in horror. "Every grain of sand in the desert? That's impossible – there are tons of them!"

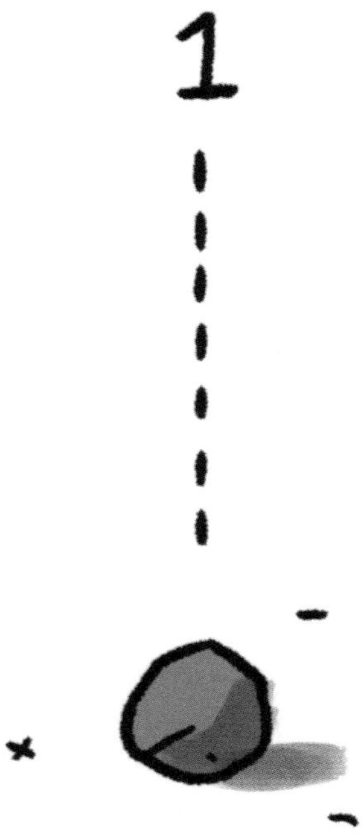
1

"But we know them all," shrieked the elf. "We remember a time when everything here was rock. Over millions of years, the rock eroded and crumbled into ever smaller stones. These stones became grains, and these grains became dust." "We? How do you mean, 'we'?" I said in amazement. "I don't see anyone else here."

The elf didn't reply, although he continued to smile. I rubbed my eyes and looked around again. Gradually, I became aware that this elf wasn't the only one in the desert. Now I saw dozens, hundreds, no thousands of such elves, wherever I looked! All were just as yellow as the sand around them, and all of them shook, rocked, curled up, flipped, whirled about in the sand. The sight of them made me dizzy; now I, too, had to close my eyes. The elf spoke, his voice like the sound of nails being pulled from wood.

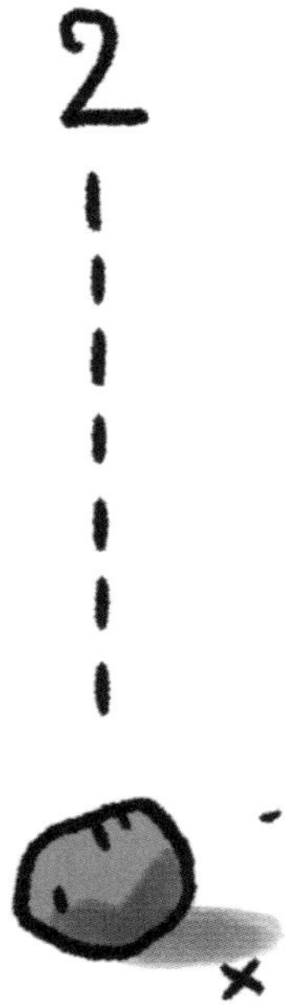
2

"We've been working here to age the desert since time immemorial. Day after day, grain by grain. So we are aware that you will never count all the grains in the desert. The number changes constantly, as grains divide and come together again. Stand quite still and you will see that the desert is constantly moving and regrouping."

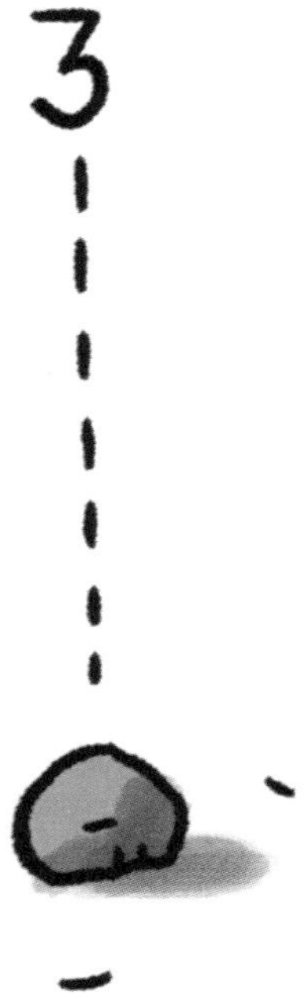
3

"But that means that nobody will ever be able to find the Cog of Time!" I cried out in despair. The elf had nothing to say to this; he closed his eyes. I waited until it seemed that he didn't mean to speak to me again. Disappointed, I turned away and walked back towards Maurice. I heard the shrill voice behind me. "It is said that the Keeper can be confused by a well-asked question."
I turned to face the elf. "Keeper?" The elf gave me a searching look. "The Keeper of the Great Cog of Time. Many adventurers have tried to outwit him. But the Keeper knows the answer to every question. Do you know what to ask him?"
"So the Cog of Time really does exist!" I rejoiced. "Who is this Keeper you speak of? And do I know what to ask him? Why should I even ask him anything?" I raved. "Where will I find him?"

The elf looked at me long and hard. Then, before my very eyes, his shape began to ripple; I blinked once and he was gone. I heard a gentle shoosh, like the sound of pouring sand, and from somewhere the elf's voice, whispering shriekily: "It's too hot in the day. Wait until nightfall."

I scanned the landscape far and wide, but there was nothing to see except Maurice and his ball. Perhaps the other elves had buried themselves in the sand, which was making its gentle shoosh sound in the breeze.

I had no idea what to do next. Exhausted, I sat down in the shade of Maurice's ball; the sun really was scorching. Thoughts flitted through my mind – of the Cog of Time, little weeping Margaret, the traitor Skim, Mum and Dad, how I would explain my running away from the farm, Uncle Remoudou – and before long I fell asleep.

The cold woke me up on my bed of damp, chilly sand. There were perhaps a million stars in the sky – I'd never seen so many. Night had fallen while I was sleeping. Maurice had wandered off into the dark with his ball. In desperation, I jumped up and called out his name into the emptiness. "Maurice! Where have you gone? Maurice the dung beetle! Please come back!"

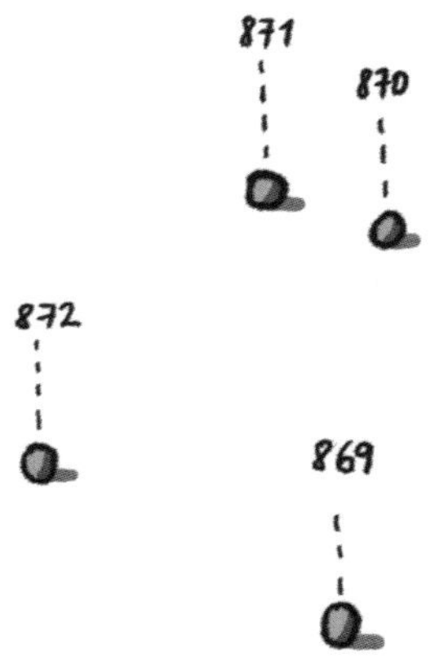

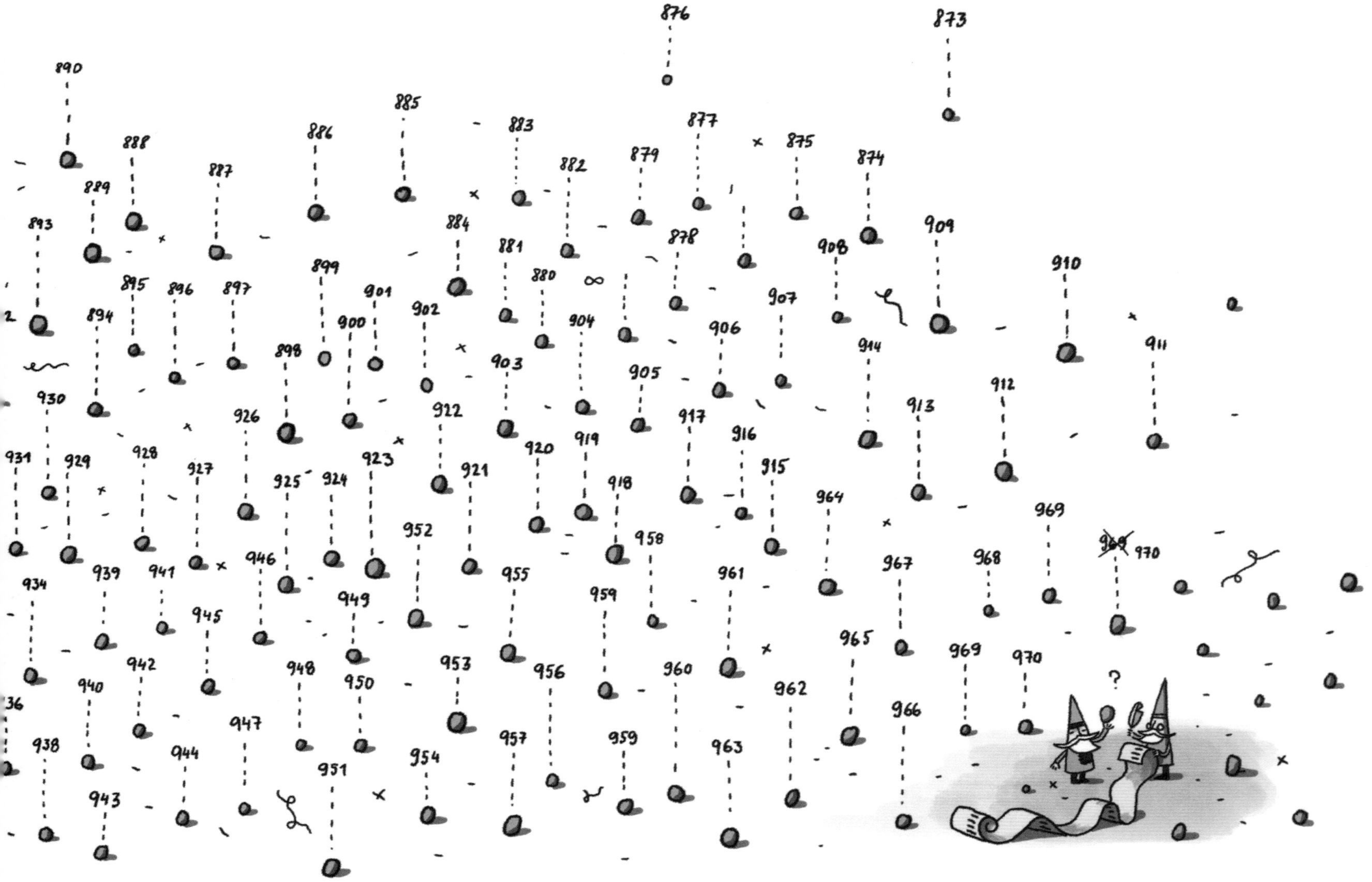

But it was all to no avail – Maurice didn't return.
Then I realized that the desert around me was
full of life. The elves who spent the day buried
in the sand were now outside and active. There
were thousands, perhaps millions, of them.
Shoosh. It was as though every grain of sand in
the desert had come to life at once. Shoosh. I had
the impression that a dune in the distance was
moving, inch by inch, like a huge slug. Shoosh.
Then, by the light of the stars, I saw a furrow
in the sand at my feet, made by Maurice's ball.
The shifting sands were already wiping it away.
I hurried along the shallow groove, clawing my
way to the top of a dune in the process. From
there, I spied Maurice in the distance; luckily,
he was moving at less than top speed.

"Maurice! Don't run away from me, my friend!"
I called to him. To my delight, he stopped
and turned towards me. When I reached him,
I realized there was a great black hole in the
sand in front of us.

Maurice prodded his ball into motion. It
descended the funnel in the sand, gathering
speed. My heart was thumping. "Is this the
place?" I asked. Then, without an answer,
Maurice and I leapt into the deep funnel in
pursuit of the ball. Down, down, down we went...

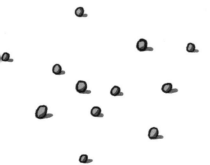

As we descended the funnel in the sand, I held onto Maurice the dung beetle for all I was worth. It was pretty scary, I can tell you. I was beginning to wonder if searching for the Cog of Time was such a good idea after all, when we reached the bottom. Suddenly the space opened up and was flooded with a strange light.

At last I was able to look around and discover where we actually were. Wow, how big it was down here! I leaned back and stared upwards and off into the distance on all sides – I'd never seen a space like this before!

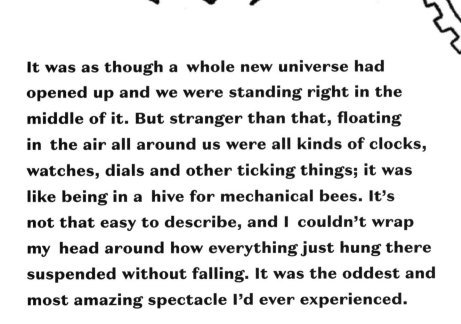

It was as though a whole new universe had opened up and we were standing right in the middle of it. But stranger than that, floating in the air all around us were all kinds of clocks, watches, dials and other ticking things; it was like being in a hive for mechanical bees. It's not that easy to describe, and I couldn't wrap my head around how everything just hung there suspended without falling. It was the oddest and most amazing spectacle I'd ever experienced.

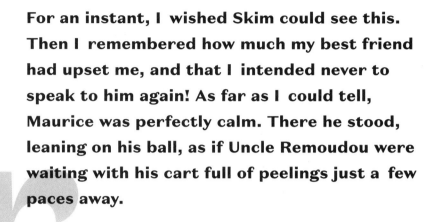

For an instant, I wished Skim could see this. Then I remembered how much my best friend had upset me, and that I intended never to speak to him again! As far as I could tell, Maurice was perfectly calm. There he stood, leaning on his ball, as if Uncle Remoudou were waiting with his cart full of peelings just a few paces away.

Suddenly a huge, gloomily terrible figure appeared at what seemed to be the very center of this endlessly ticking space. Where its head should have been, this figure had a massive hourglass. Each time it moved, the sand moved from the upper chamber of the glass to the lower, making the same shooshing sound as it did in the desert. It took me a while to notice that grains of sand in the hourglass formed something like a mouth and eyes, and that these eyes were fixed on me. Shoosh! I was shaking with cold, and fear. Besides that, I was thirsty and had a sudden urge to use the bathroom at the same time.

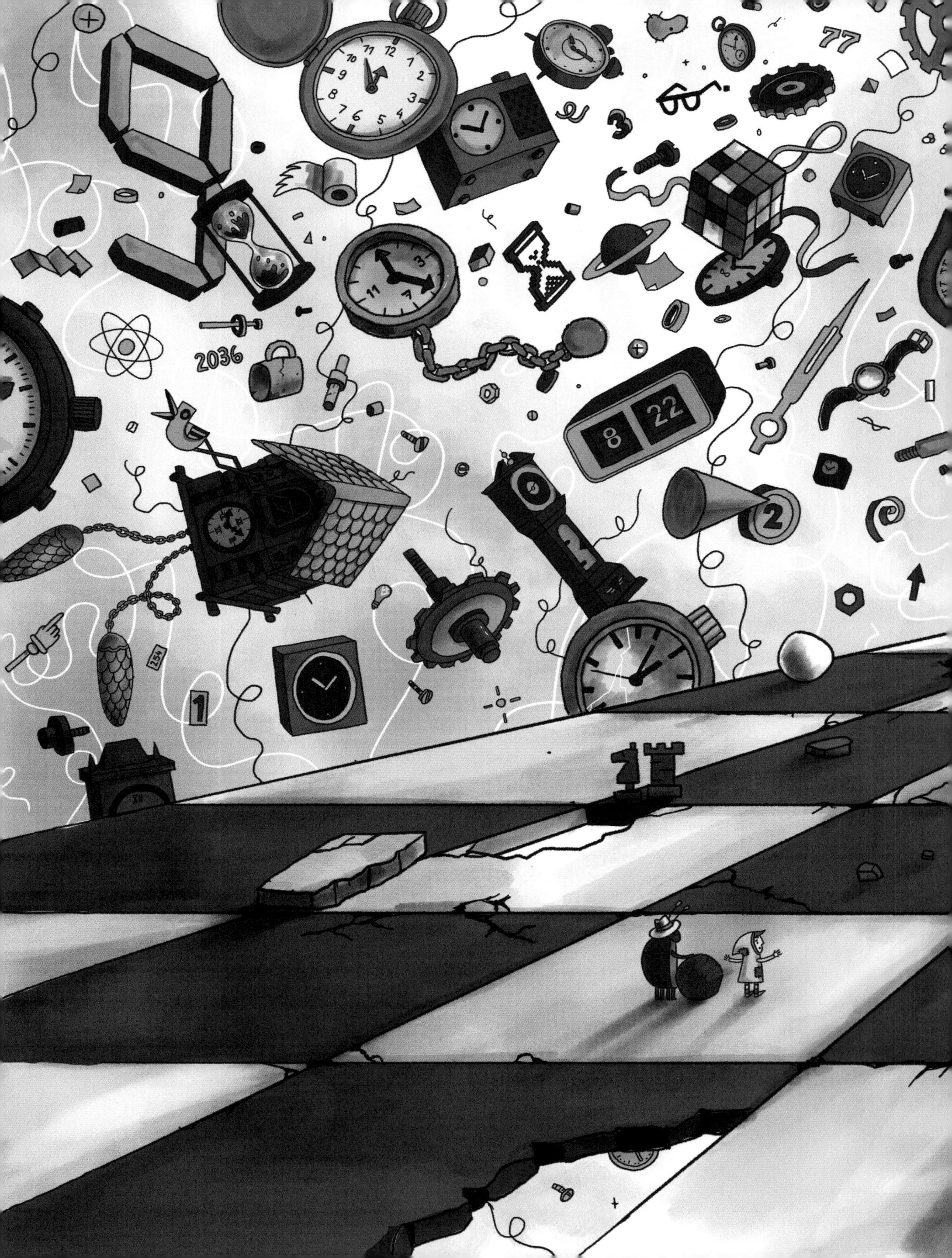

77
2036
8
22

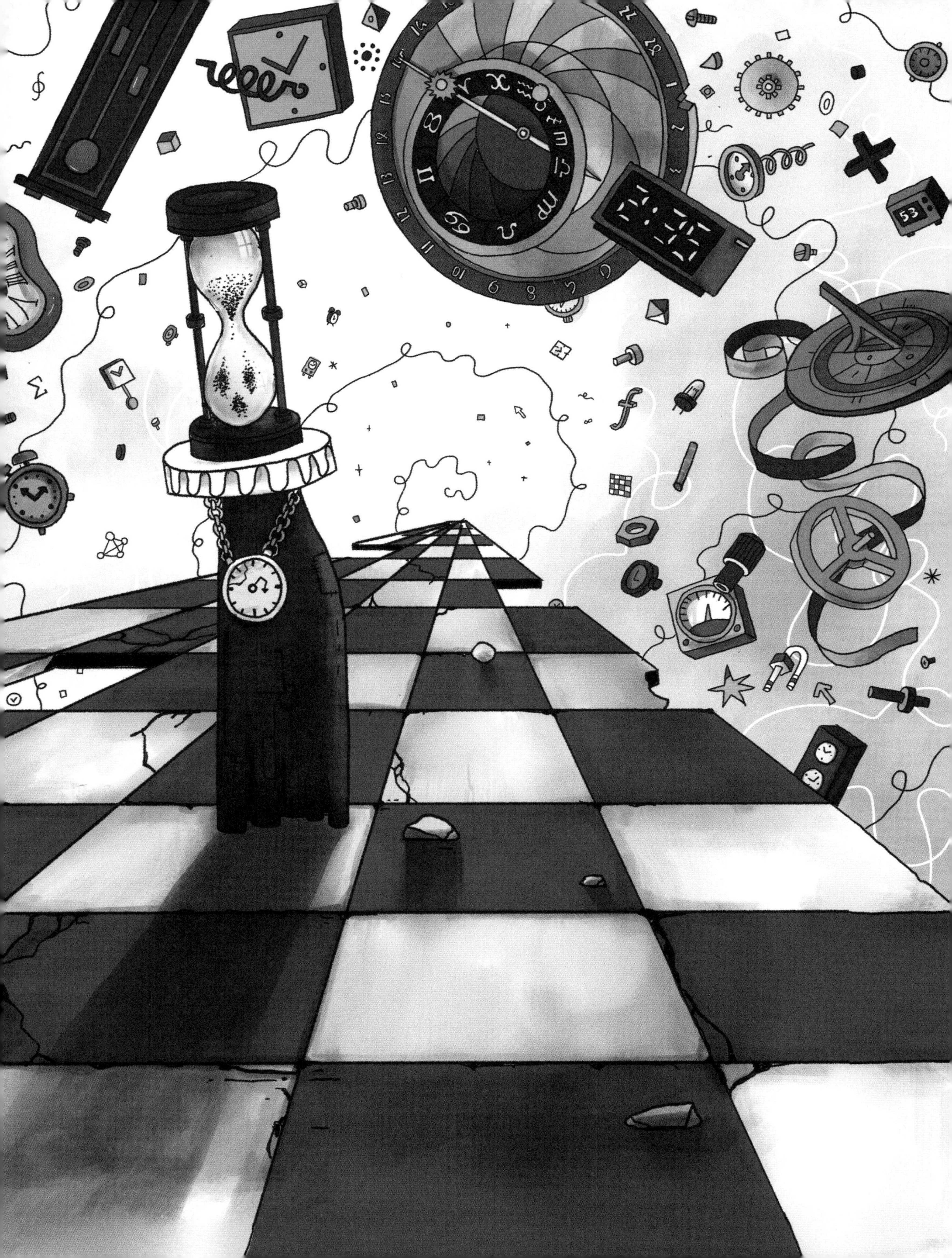
53

The tall figure stood still and silent but for the constant pouring of the sand and the gloomy murmur this made. When at last it spoke, the figure's voice was deep. "What do you want here, Typo?" Wow, he knew my name! I couldn't imagine anything more terrifying, but at that time I had no idea what was coming. Trying to be heroic, I answered the giant in the strongest voice I could muster, with an awkward formality. "Hello, sir. I seek the Cog of Time. It pleases me that you know my name. May I ask who *you* are?" "Shoosh! I am the Great Keeper of the Great and Almighty Cog of Time. I know the name of everyone from the day they are born. I have been on guard here since time immemorial. I may let no one – and I mean NO ONE – pass. Turn around and go back the way you came."

So we've reached the end of the road, I told myself sadly. It seemed that we had trudged all this way in vain. The Great Keeper told us, "Enough, you may go no further", and we were powerless to object. How foolish I'd been to think that by stealing Maurice the dung beetle and having him lead me to the Cog of Time, I'd be able to put a stop to all aging as easily as changing ABC to ACB! That it should all end like this, though? No, I couldn't let that happen.

Frantically I considered what to do. And while I was thinking, I noticed something highly interesting. Maurice was completely absorbed by chasing his ball, and I wondered if the Keeper had even noticed him; his eyes of sand looked at me and me only. Suddenly Maurice sprung forward and simply walked past the Keeper, and the Keeper did nothing! Unable to contain my surprise, I called Maurice's name.

Shoosh. "Who are you talking to?" boomed the Keeper, and the stream of sand in his head quickened. Yes, the Keeper really had addressed only me the whole time. It was quite possible that Maurice was invisible to him. "Why, Maurice the dung beetle, of course!" I said craftily. "He's over there!" I pointed at Maurice, who was standing behind the Keeper, cleaning an antenna with a nonchalant leg. Shoosh. The Keeper turned this way and that in confusion. "Dung beetle? I don't see anyone at all! Are you making fun of me, entropic elf Typo? Are you trying to trick me in order to get to the Great Cog of Time? If so, you will never succeed. Shoosh."

So it was true – the Keeper couldn't see Maurice. How amazing! I was beginning to realize that Uncle Remoudou hadn't been making it up when he'd said that the Cog of Time had no power over dung beetles. Still, although Maurice was invisible to the Keeper, he could see me perfectly well. When I made a slight move, he stepped briskly in front of me and boomed, "You're going NOWHERE! Access to the Great Cog of Time is forbidden! I shall not tell you again. Shoosh."

Then I remembered the words of the desert elf: The Keeper can be confused by a well-asked question. I had noticed that the sand in the hourglass that served as the Keeper's head streamed wildly whenever he was confused or called upon to think hard. And I remembered how we had labored over Professor Block's question about the chicken and the egg, and how Badegg had claimed that when an egg hatches, the chicken that comes out of it is actually a spoiled egg.

"WHAT THE EYES OF THE KEEPER DO NOT SEE, DOES NOT HARM THE COG OF TIME."
ANCIENT DUNG BEETLE PROVERB

At that moment I had to admit that perhaps my dad had been right to say I should always listen well to Professor Block, as he had much to teach me. I looked straight into the swirling, trickling eyes and said, "I'm sorry, sir. I wished neither to trick nor annoy you. All I wanted was to ask you something. This problem has troubled me for a long time. As your knowledge is so deep and wide and profound, perhaps you'll be able to help me. Then I'll turn around and return to where I came from, as you wish."

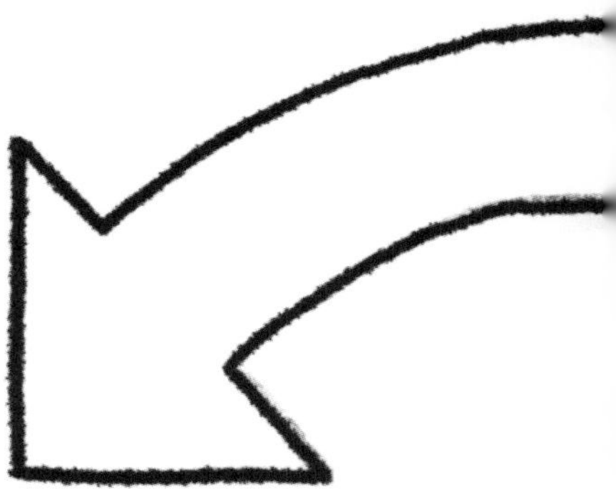

"Shoosh. I'm not here to answer everybody's questions," said the Keeper angrily. "Ask your questions at school. My only job is to protect the Cog of Time."

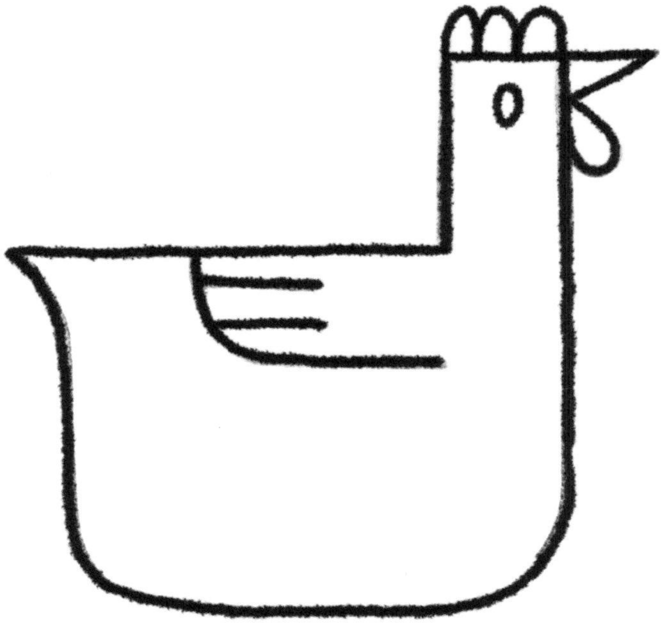

"But we weren't able to answer this question at school," I shouted, sounding as desperate as I could. "Professor Block said nobody has ever been able to answer this question. He said it's impossible." "Every question has an answer. Shoosh. I know Block. He's a young elf who moves letters around in books, I believe." "Professor Block is six hundred years old." "Shoosh. Indeed, a mere youngster. No wonder he struggles to answer simple questions."

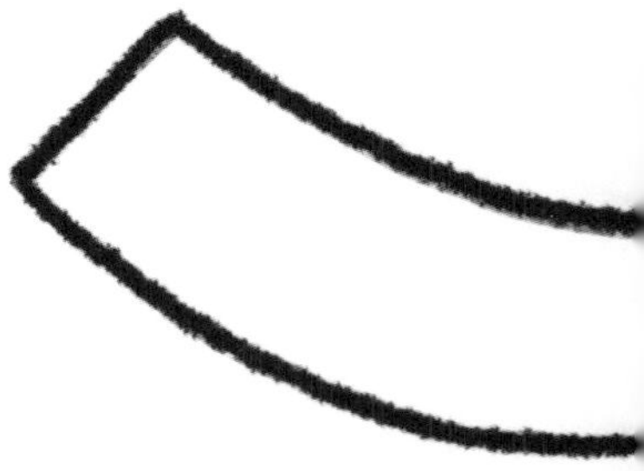

“You’d know the answer, though, wouldn’t you?” I persisted. “I always know the answer!” boomed the Keeper. “But there is nothing for you here. If you do not leave immediately, I will bring the most fearful sandstorm down on you!” As I cowered before him in pretend terror, he seemed to revel in my fear of him. Then, as I'd hoped, he gave in. “Very well, then, what was your question? Ask it then go. Shoosh.” I took a deep breath before stating energetically:

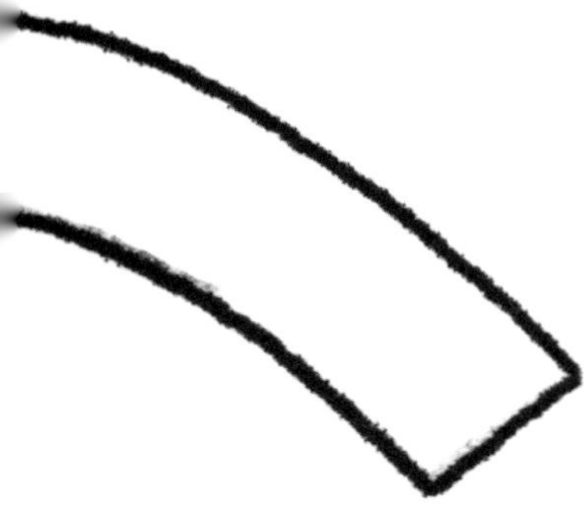

“WHICH CAME FIRST – THE CHICKEN OR THE EGG?”

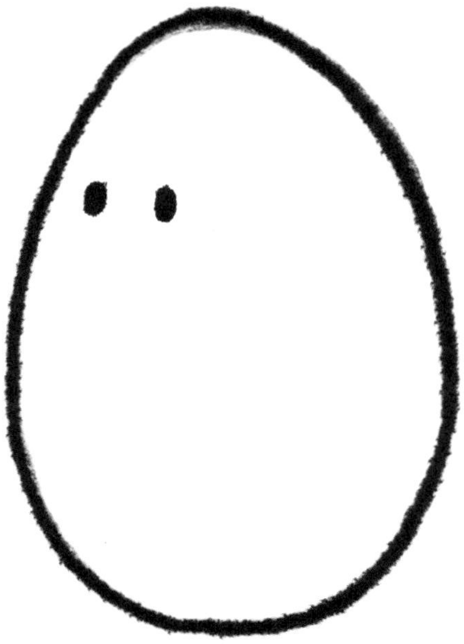

Shoosh. Shoo-oosh. Shoo-oo-oosh. The sand-headed Keeper went at it at full tilt. “It is indeed a good question. I know the answer, of course. I know all answers. Shoosh. The chicken must hatch from the egg. So the egg must come before the chicken. Shoosh. But who lays the egg? Why, the chicken, of course! Shoosh. So the chicken must come first, and then the egg—shoosh—the egg—shoosh ...”

As the Keeper struggled in vain to answer the Professor’s special question, I saw his eyes dissolve in a rush of sand.

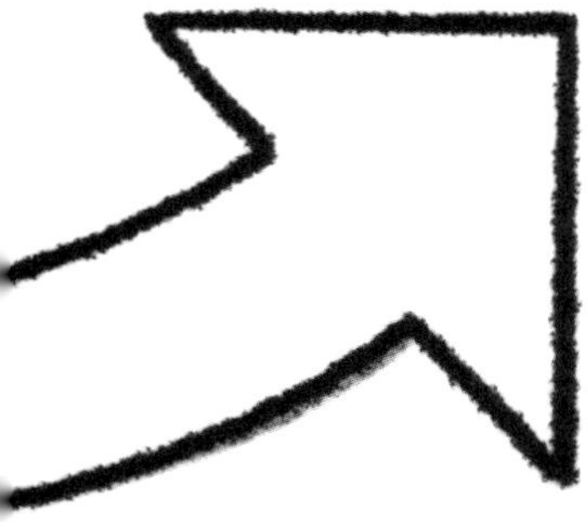

At this point, the Keeper forgot all about me. Maurice pricked up his antennae and went on. The path to the Cog of Time was open. I took a deep breath and ran after Maurice.

THE QUESTION OF THE CHICKEN AND THE EGG

A TEAM OF SCIENTISTS CALLED HOOVER, SLURPER AND LIPSMACK HAS ADVANCED THE THEORY THAT THIS ENDURING PROBLEM CAN BE SOLVED BY ANSWERING ANOTHER QUESTION FIRST: WHICH IS BETTER FOR BREAKFAST – AN OMELETTE OR A HARD-BOILED EGG? RESEARCH IS STILL ONGOING. SO FAR, RESULTS SUGGEST EITHER ONE OR THE OTHER.

13:

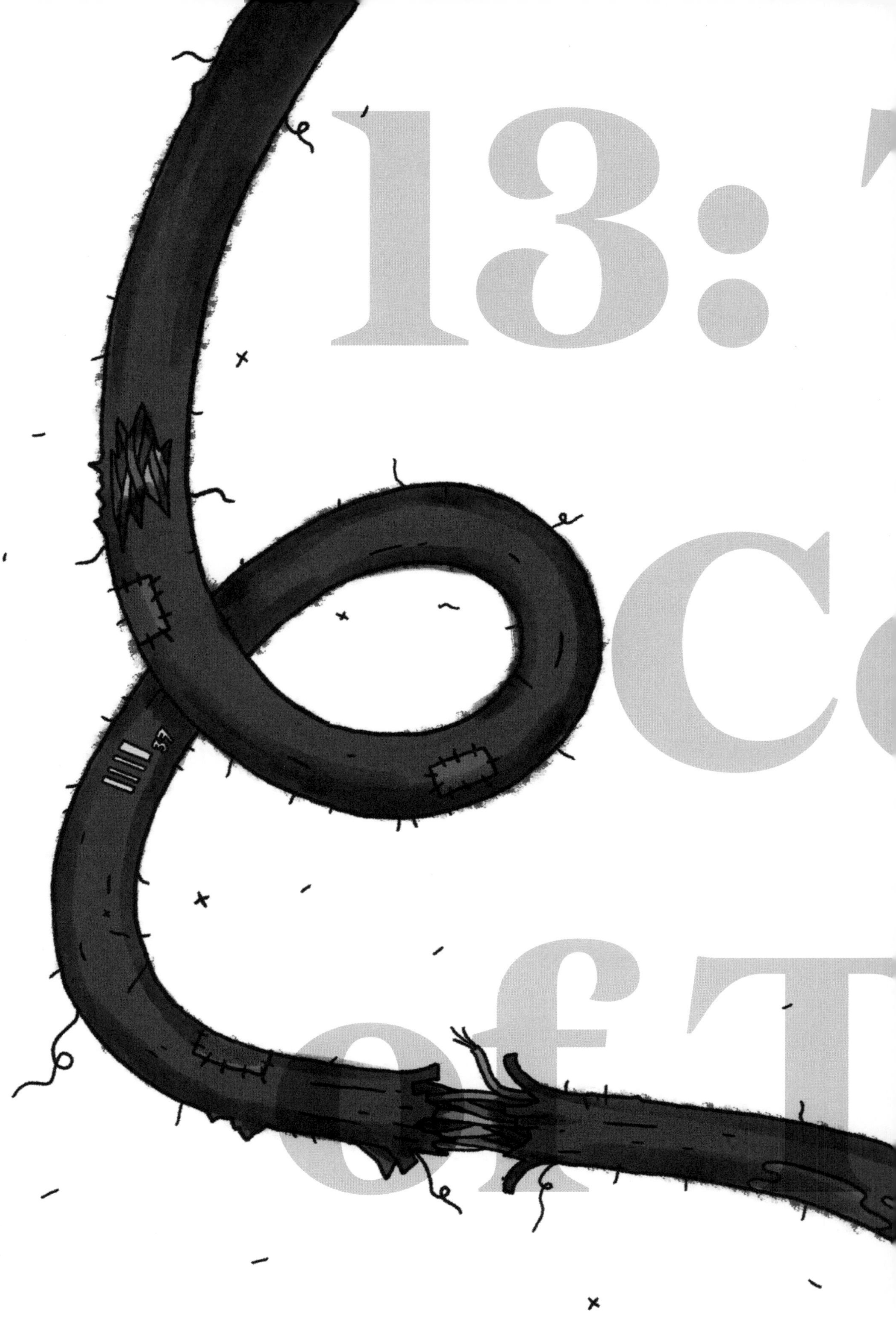

It's tough for me to explain what happened next. As the Cog of Time is extremely difficult to reach, I'm assuming that no one reading this has ever seen it. But if by any chance you or your parents know someone who has, I suggest you ask them about it: they will help you understand better what I'm about to tell you. Even now, I don't fully understand what happened. In the end, I don't mind telling you straight out, I really did succeed in putting a stop to all aging. But something weird happened, too. In fact, lots of weird things happened. So let me start at the beginning.

At the beginning, I headed for the end. But as I followed Maurice deeper and deeper into that vast mysterious space, for a while I thought there would be no end. In the strange, bright, flickering light – it was a bit like looking at the night-sky in the desert – we were surrounded by clocks, watches and other things whose functions were a mystery to me. There were other moments when I felt I was walking among the stars.

Then I saw Maurice, standing at a place where everything seemed to come together, forming a wall that barred the way. Although all came to an end there, at the same time it was still everywhere around. (I told you it would be difficult to describe.) Anyway, Maurice was standing next to a great lever that was sticking out of something. "I have brought you all the way to the Cog of Time, Typo," he said. "I hope you are glad." I gasped.

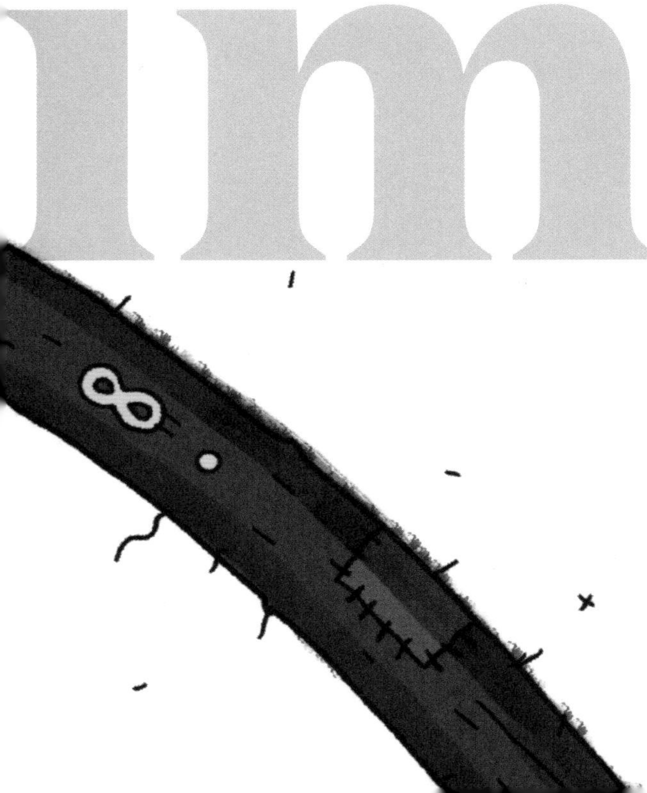

Cog of Time? Nothing I could see bore the slightest resemblance to anything like a cog. And where had that strange lever come from? And most of all, the dung beetle had spoken – what the heck?!

"Yes, I can talk," said Maurice, quite unruffled. "All scarabs can talk. It's true what they say about us. When the world came into being, we learned about reincarnation – how to make ourselves born again. When we die, we are reborn out of what is left of us. It's not all that difficult, but it's important not to be squeamish about what comes out of you."

Here was Maurice talking like a book, while I was unable to utter a single word, such was my surprise. Maurice pointed a leg at the lever and said, "Anyway, if you want to put a stop to aging, that's what this lever is for. I must warn you, though – once it's done, it can't be reversed."

I managed to swallow and ask: "But Dung Beet—I mean, Maurice, does this mean you've used the lever before?" Maurice shook his head. "No. Why? I've no need to put a stop to aging. I just knew where the lever was, you wanted me to take you to it, so I did. By the way, it wouldn't hurt you to thank me..."

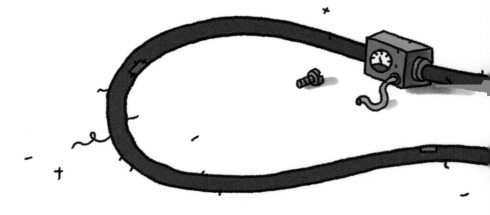

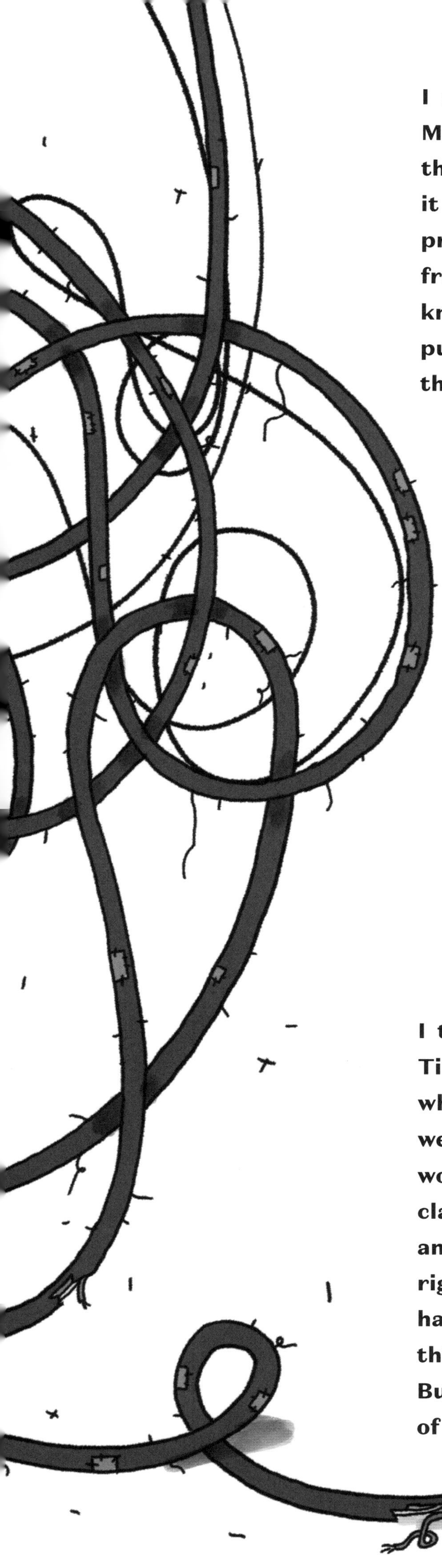

I remembered my manners. “You’re right, Maurice. Thank you very much. This is the very thing I wanted. It’s just that ... I wasn’t expecting it to be a lever.” Maurice yawned. “What’s the problem with a lever?” I thought this over frantically. “There isn’t one, or ... Well, I don’t know. It just looks terribly simple to me. I just pull a lever and the job is done!” “That’s the best thing about levers,” Maurice said with approval.

I went over to the lever and took a good look at it. It looked just like any other lever. I turned back to Maurice. “So what exactly will happen if I pull it?” I asked. “You’ll stop the Cog of Time,” replied Maurice with an air of unconcern, as if it were of no more significance than snapping off a light. I wasn’t going to let him off so easily. “So where is the Cog of Time?” “My dear Typo, the Cog of Time is all around us!” said Maurice, as he calmly adjusted his antennae and puffed his pipe. Again I looked this way and that, but all I saw was the lever. Aha, I thought, the Cog of Time must be on the other end of the wire that leads out of the lever. So if Maurice was right, it would be enough for me to give the lever a shove.

I thought for a moment. By stopping the Cog of Time, I would put a stop to aging. Wasn’t that what I wanted? If I did it, Margaret would never weep for her broken toys again. Professor Block would finally have to close his History of Aging classes. The squealer Skim, Mrs Frosting, Mum and Dad – all of them would see that I had been right; what’s more, they would thank me. They’d have loads and loads of time to... to... Well, I’d think about what they were going to do later. But there would be lots of time to do all kinds of things.

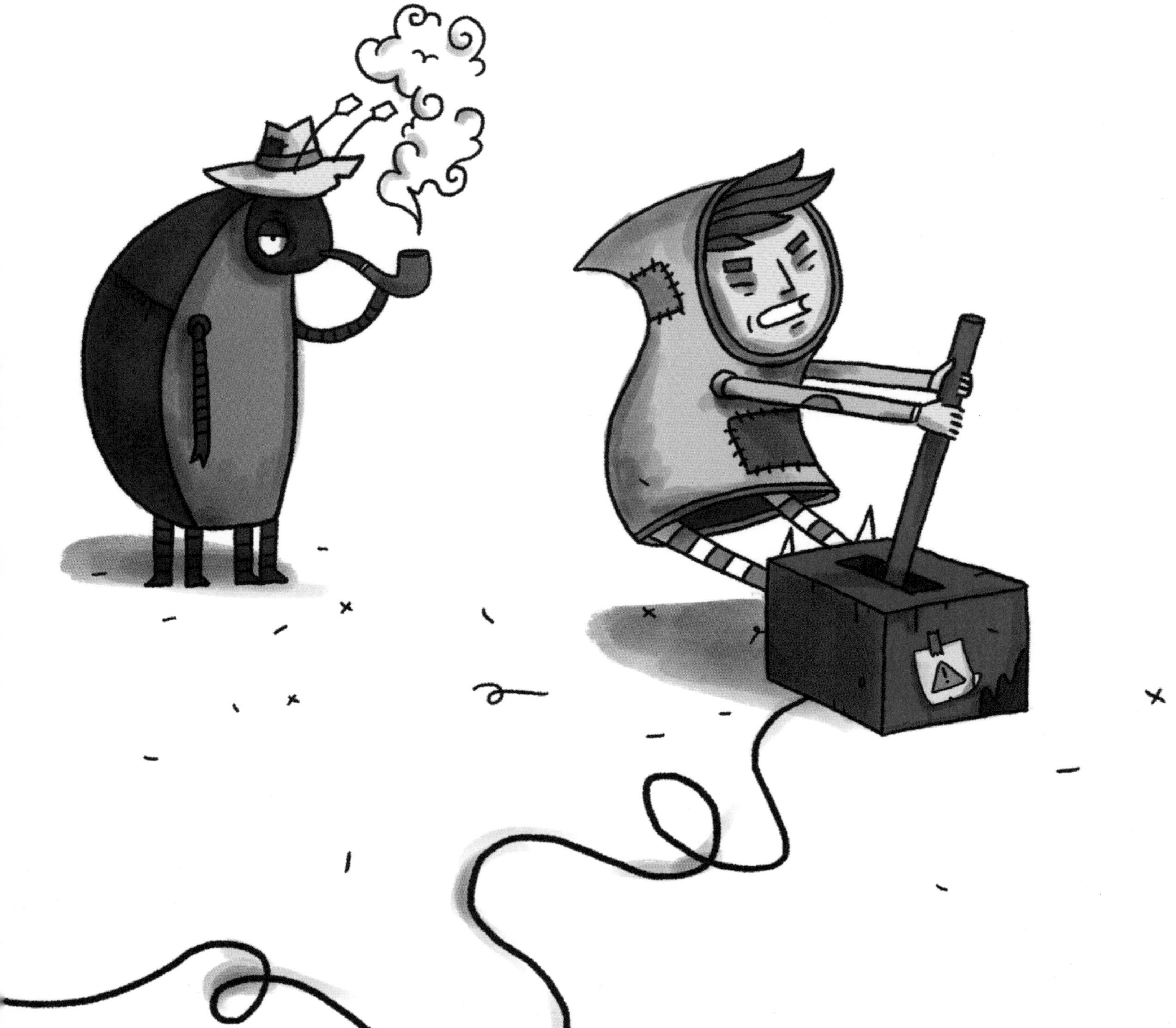

As I grasped the lever with both hands, again I had a fleeting image of Margaret's tear-stained face at her birthday party. Putting a stop to aging was surely the right thing to do, I told myself.

I pulled the lever.

AND SUDDENLY ... NOTHING.

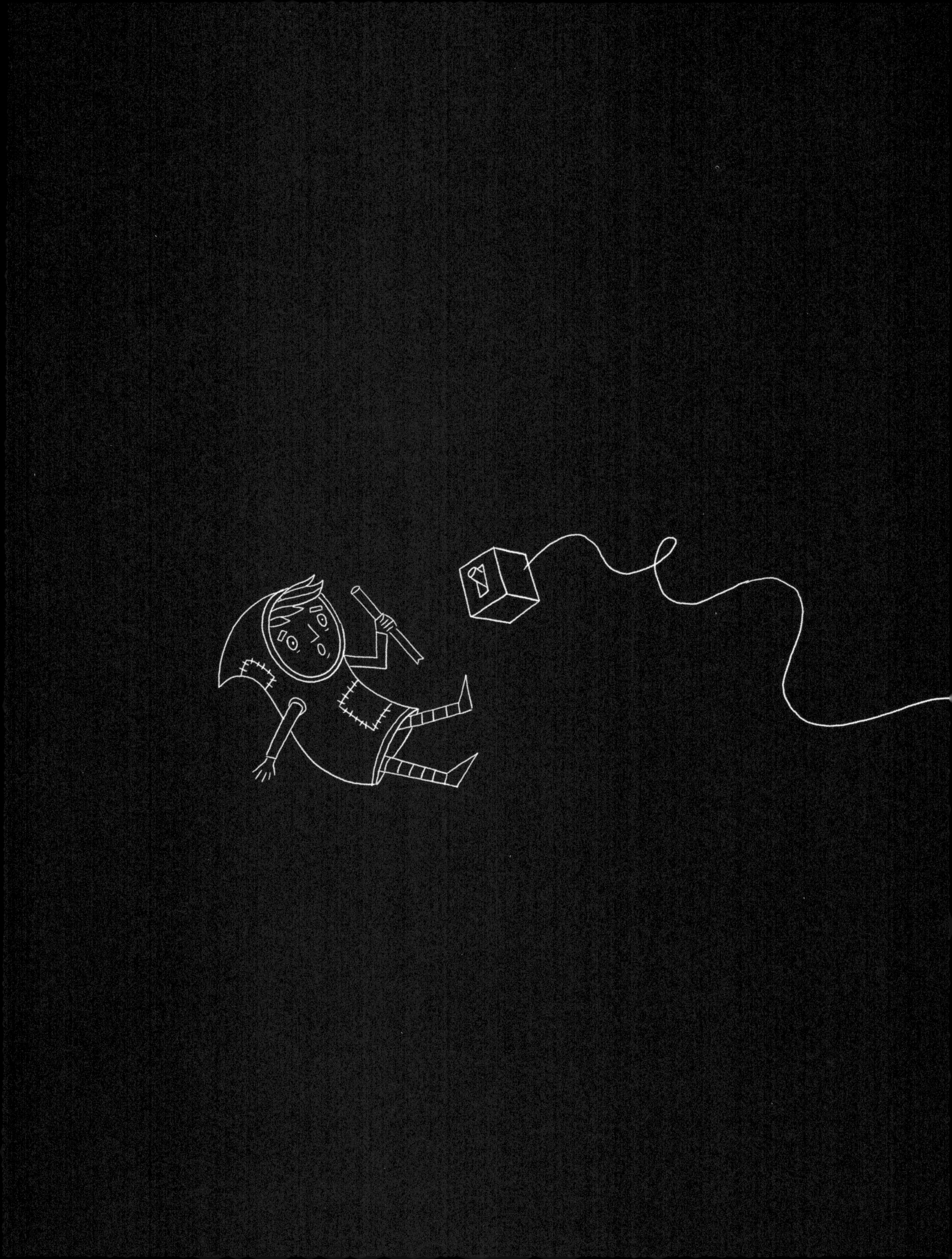

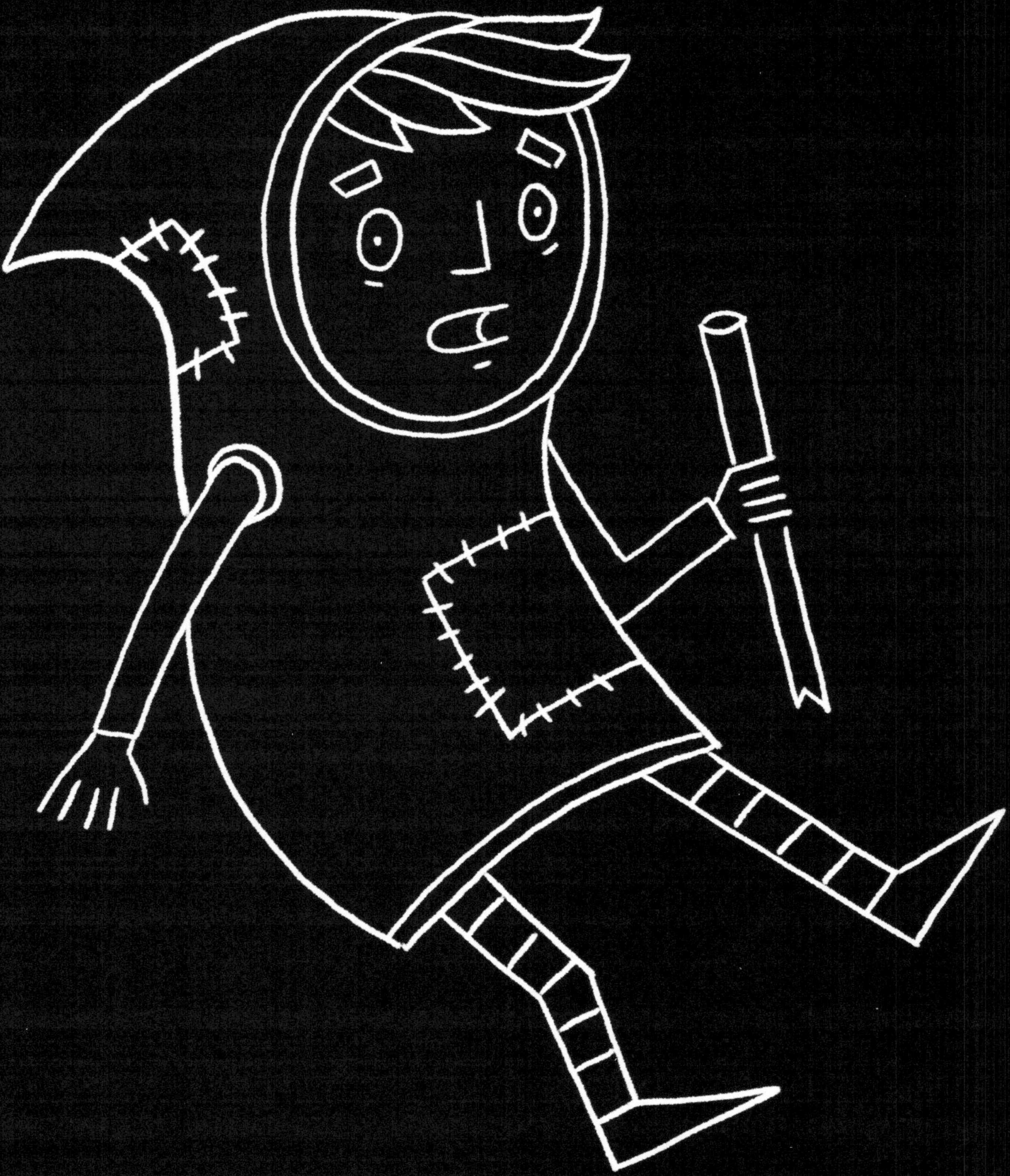

NOT A THING. ANYWHERE.

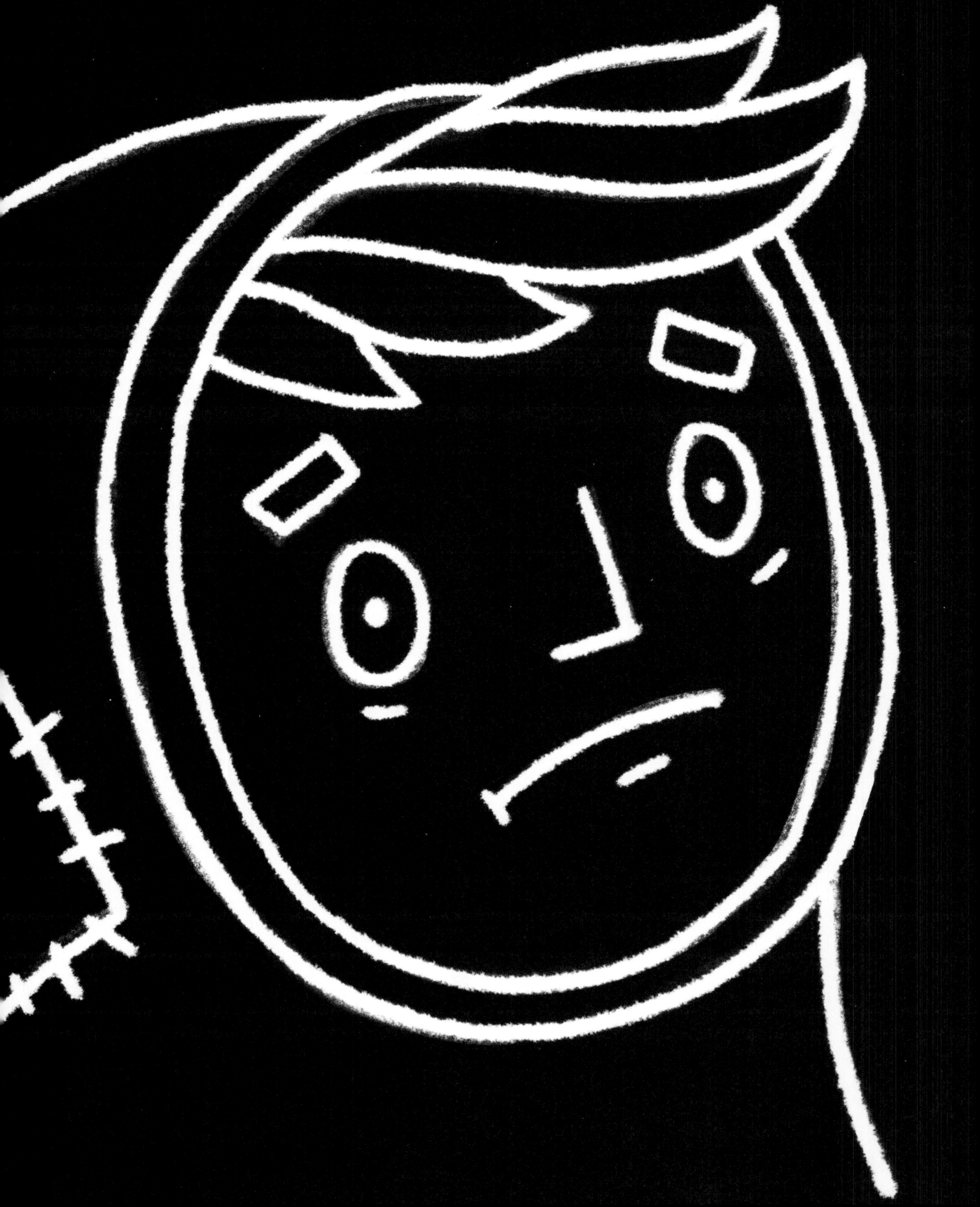

NOT A SINGLE, BLESSED THING!

I don't know how best to describe it to you. When I pulled
that lever, everything just vanished. The eerie light
vanished, the clocks and stars vanished. All we were left
with was pitch black. Maurice, the lever and I were just
hovering in some kind of void. At least that's how it seemed,
because otherwise there was nothing. We might have been
hovering; we might just as well have been at the bottom or
the top of something. It was completely disorienting.

"What's happened, Maurice?" I said in a choked voice.
"You've put a stop to aging," he replied. "You've frozen
time. Everything that was in progress or development is
now at a standstill. There's no light because light waves are
no longer in motion. The Cog of Time has stopped. Nothing
is getting any older. Nothing is moving. There is nothing."
"But I didn't want for there to be nothing! All I wanted was
for things to stop aging!" "And your wish has come true.
Things that don't exist, don't age. You did it! Rejoice!"

But I didn't feel in the least like rejoicing. I was
stunned by what had happened. Perhaps you are,
too, as you read this. Maurice was cool, calm and
collected, but I was close to tears. I didn't at
all like the fact that nothing was all there was –
I mean that there wasn't anything, anywhere and
that I was all alone in the dark but for a talking
dung beetle. I wanted my mom and my dad;
I wanted Skim and Uncle Remoudou; I wouldn't
even have minded the company of Pryer, or
Wormold and Badegg.

ANYONE AT ALL
would have done!

I tried returning the lever to its original position but
I couldn't. So I tugged at it as hard as I could – and
it broke off! As I stared at the now useless lever in my
hand, Maurice pricked up his antennae. "I told you that
it couldn't be reversed," he said, as if that was that.

"But that's impossible!" And now I really did burst
into tears. "But there must be a way!" I cried. "The
two of us are still here, aren't we?" Maurice nodded.
"We're beyond the influence of the Cog of Time. You,
because you're the one who stopped it, me because
I know how to be. But everything else has stopped."
"If I'd known that there's nothing without aging,
I would never have stopped the Cog of Time! Why
didn't you tell me this would happen!" "You never
asked. But don't cry, Typo. Nothingness isn't so bad,
really. I've been through it a few times, and I've
always emerged from it as if reborn! That said, this is
a rather different case, because you've stopped aging
altogether. So it's likely to last longer this time. I'd
say approximately forever, ha-ha! So I'm going to take
a little nap. Night-night." Whereupon the terrible
creature yawned, rolled over onto his wing cases,
began to snore and drifted away, I knew not where.

What else can I tell you except that I was more
distraught than I'd ever been. Appalled by what I'd
done, I cried floods and floods of tears. If you've
ever been at home alone all night, or waited alone
in a car for someone who doesn't come for ages,
or found yourself indefinitely in a place where
there's no one else, you know that solitude quickly
gets difficult to bear. Some people can't be on their
own for a second; others can put up with solitude
for quite a long time. But no one can put up with
it FOREVER! Imagine such a thing. I did.

The very worst thing about nothingness was that it
surrounded me. There was no way of getting out of it. In
order not to be bothered by this, you probably have to be
a dung beetle. Just when I was starting to think that all this
would drive me mad, I heard a thin voice from somewhere
in the distance. "Hello-o-o? Is anyone there? Hello-o-o?"
I couldn't believe my ears. This was a voice I knew very well ...

14: Af out now

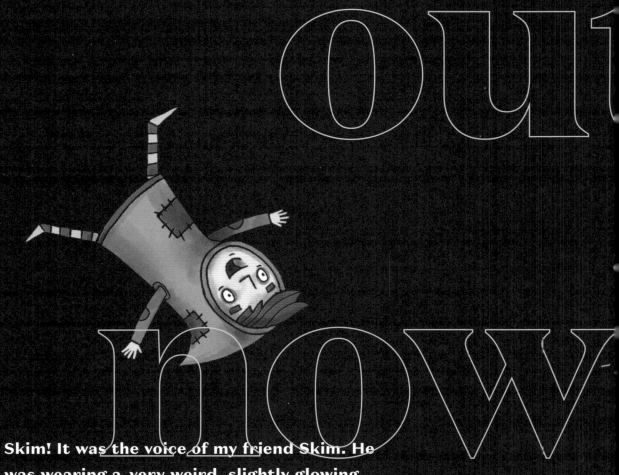

Skim! It was the voice of my friend Skim. He was wearing a very weird, slightly glowing outfit and waving his arms and legs about as he approached. Never in my life had I been so glad to see his dim & grubby face. When you're at your lowest ebb and a friend appears literally out of nowhere, the feeling of delight is incomparable.

riend
t of
here

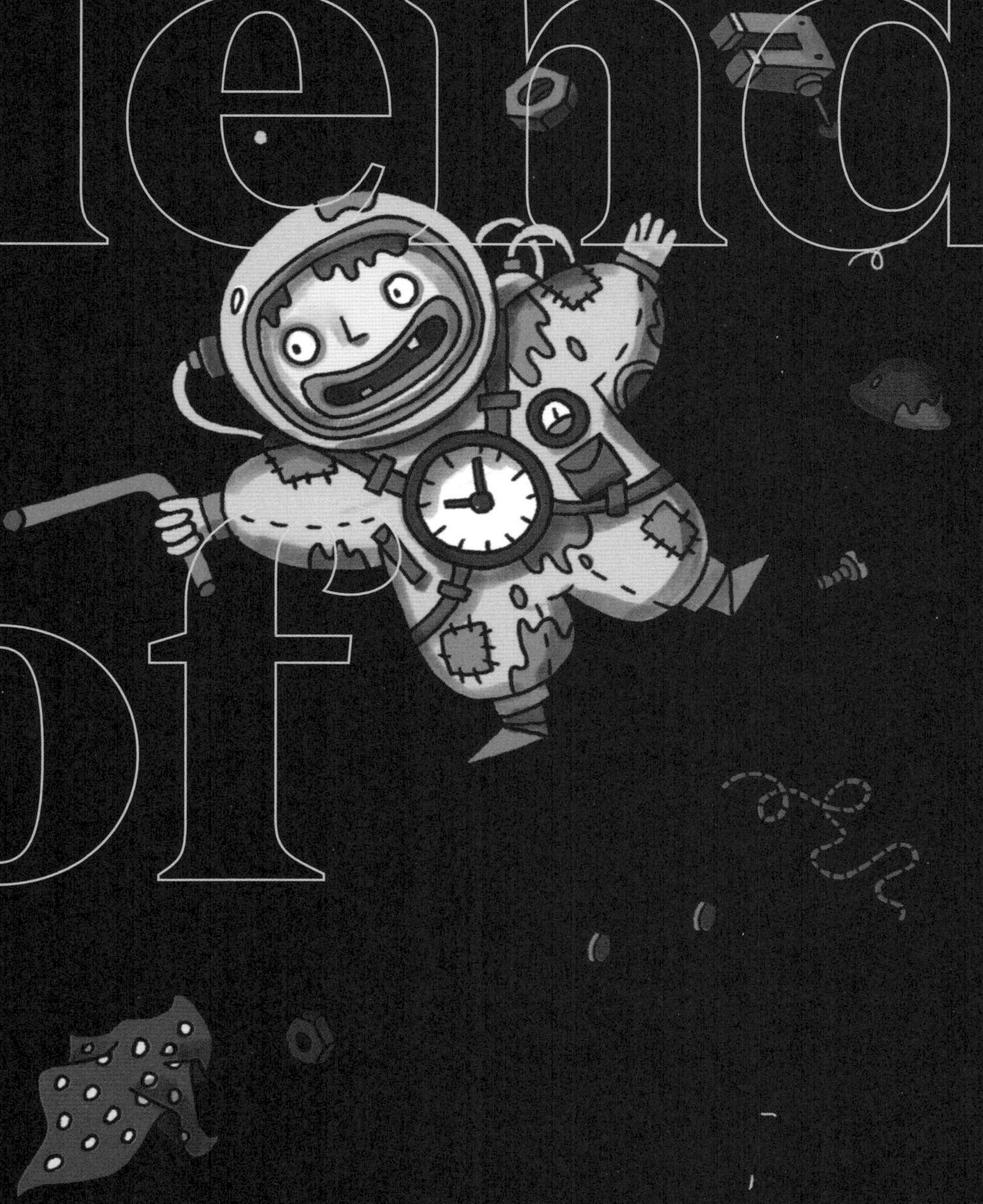

"Skim! Here! Over here!" I yelled and thrashed my arms and legs about in the darkness. He spotted me at last and he steered himself towards me. Then we literally fell into each other's arms. "Skim!" "Typo! I'm so glad to see you, old buddy old pal!" We hugged and patted each other on the back, laughing hard. How great it was not to be all alone in the pitch-black nothingness! But I couldn't understand why Skim was wearing such a strange outfit. Then it dawned on me. "Blinkin' heck, Skim – you're wearing the chrono pressure suit!"

I thought I couldn't see anything because of h
fast my head was spinning," said Skim in a sha
voice. "But when my head stopped spinning,
still I saw nothing at all. I tell you, buddy, that
was the scariest thing that has ever happened
to me!" "Tell me about it!" I said. "I'm so glad
to see you here!"

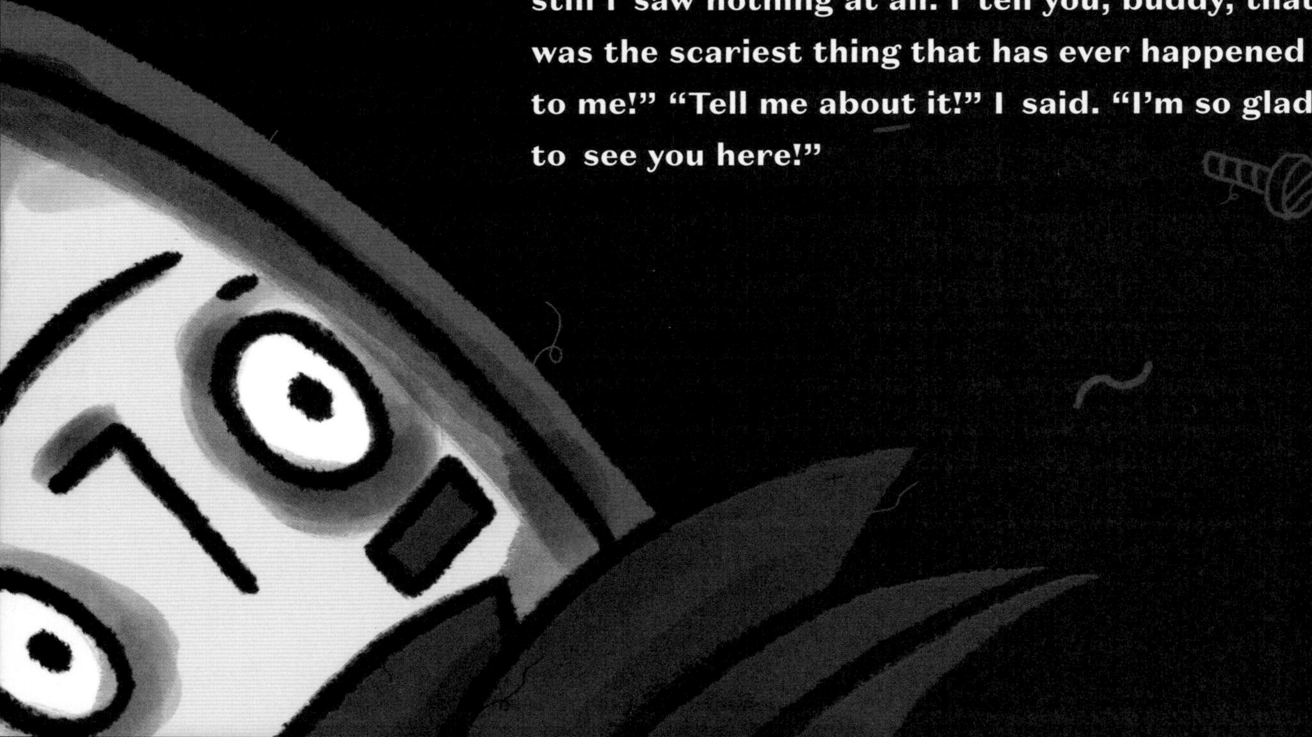

Skim gave me a questioning look. "So you don't mind that I gave you away?" I hugged him again. "Don't be silly, Skim! We're friends, and I know that you meant well. Besides, we can't fall out now, when the only folk left in the world are the two of us and an annoying dung beetle."

"I'm so glad, Typo. I was so worried you wouldn't want to be my friend anymore." Skim stopped talking and looked about in the dark. "I don't suppose you know what happened?" he asked anxiously.

So I explained it all to my great friend Skim. I told him about Maurice and our trip around the world at breakneck speed. I told him about the elves of the desert and the Great Keeper, and how I'd pulled the lever and stopped the Cog of Time. "Cocoa-loco!"

How else would you expect Skim to react? But while he was expressing amazement, my brain was working overtime. "You know what this means, Skim, don't you?" I said. "Littlehand's chrono pressure suit really works!" "Wow – you're right!" said Skim, scratching his helmet. "If it didn't, I wouldn't be here right now, would I?" "That's right!" I agreed. "The Cog of Time lost its power over you. So when I switched it off, nothing happened to you. Dr Littlehand is a lot brainier that we all thought." "Still, what are we going to do, Typo? Are things going to stay like this forever?" "Of course not! We'll put everything right, you'll see." Thanks to the appearance of my friend, I was feeling unexpectedly strong. Together, I thought, we would solve this problem as we solved those Professor Blunder assigned us, although this one was far more difficult.

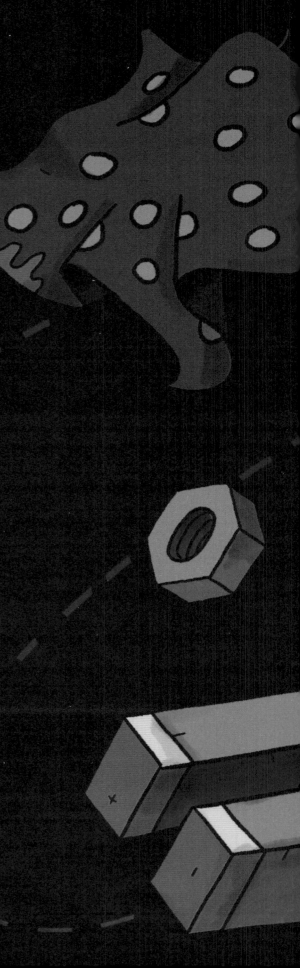

Skim and I pounced on the broken lever and subjected it to a thorough inspection. We pushed and hammered at it in vain: it was too broken to push back into position. We recalled all the tricks we'd ever heard about from the elves who worked on decomposition, corrosion and disintegration – again in vain. In the end we flopped down in the void next to the lever, exhausted. We wondered what our world would be like, now that there was nothing but nothing.

'It's all Maurice's fault, you know," I muttered angrily. "Why is it Maurice's fault?" asked Skim, surprised. "Because he brought me here, he put me up to moving the lever, and he didn't tell me about all that would happen if I did. "So Maurice really can talk?" said Skim, again in amazement. At this, my patience snapped. "Yes, yes, he can talk! But let's not talk about him now. I've had about as much of that puffed-up, idiot dung beetle as I can take."

"Are you speaking about me, gentlemen?" It was Maurice, of course. He had emerged from behind the lever, just as I was calling him a puffed-up, idiot dung beetle. I know, of course, that you can say something about someone that you don't want them to hear and they surprise you by appearing at that very moment. But that this should happen out of nowhere when nowhere was all there was! How's that for bad luck?

Fortunately, though, Maurice didn't seem at all put out. Skim was obviously delighted to see him. "Maurice, my friend! How great it is to see you!" he gabbled. "So you can talk! That's cocoa-loco! My uncle misses you terribly, you know."

"I miss him, too," said Maurice unhappily. "That dump is one of the nicest places I've ever known, anywhere in the world." "Well," said Skim, "if you help us out, you could take yourself back there. Nice dung balls to be had there."

I thought it best to stay silent... Maurice appeared to think about this. For a long time he examined the lever in silence. Then his antennae bobbed back and forth; he was nodding his head. "To get the Cog of Time working again," he said, "you'd need the right crank and a great deal of luck!"

This beetle was really beginning to get on my nerves. "Thanks so much for your advice, Maurice!" I said, voice dripping with sarcasm, making Maurice grimace. Then I noticed that Skim was wriggling about in his pressure suit.

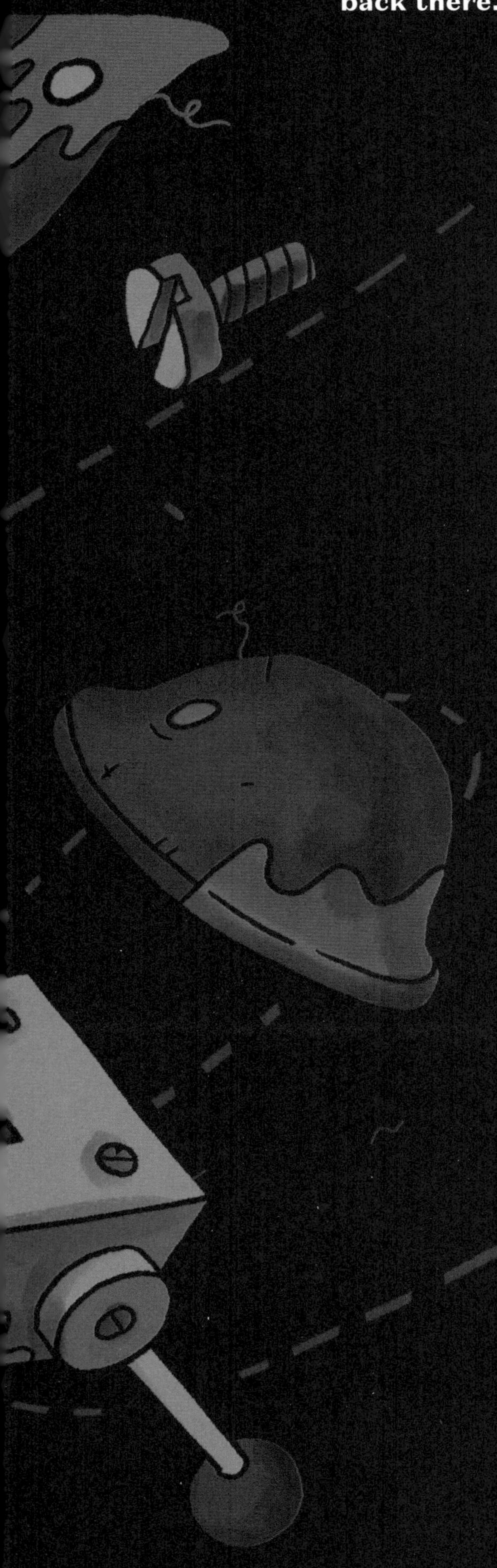

"What are you doing, Skim?" "I'm sure I had it in here somewhere ..." said Skim, as he continued to fidget in his suit. "There was a pretty big pocket in here with lots of things in it ..." "Surely you're not taking that crazy dung beetle seriously?" I said, shaking my head. By now Skim was pulling out the things Dr Littlehand had left in the suit's pocket – a pocket knife-blunter, a pre-sucked rum chocolate candy, a few nuts and bolts, a used paper handkerchief and – a crank! "Hey, look what we've got!" cried Skim in triumph.

I was about to tell him to leave that nonsense alone – didn't we have a world to save? But then I got a good look at the crank. "S-Skim! B-buddy!" I gasped. "That crank is exactly the same size the lever was before I broke it off!"

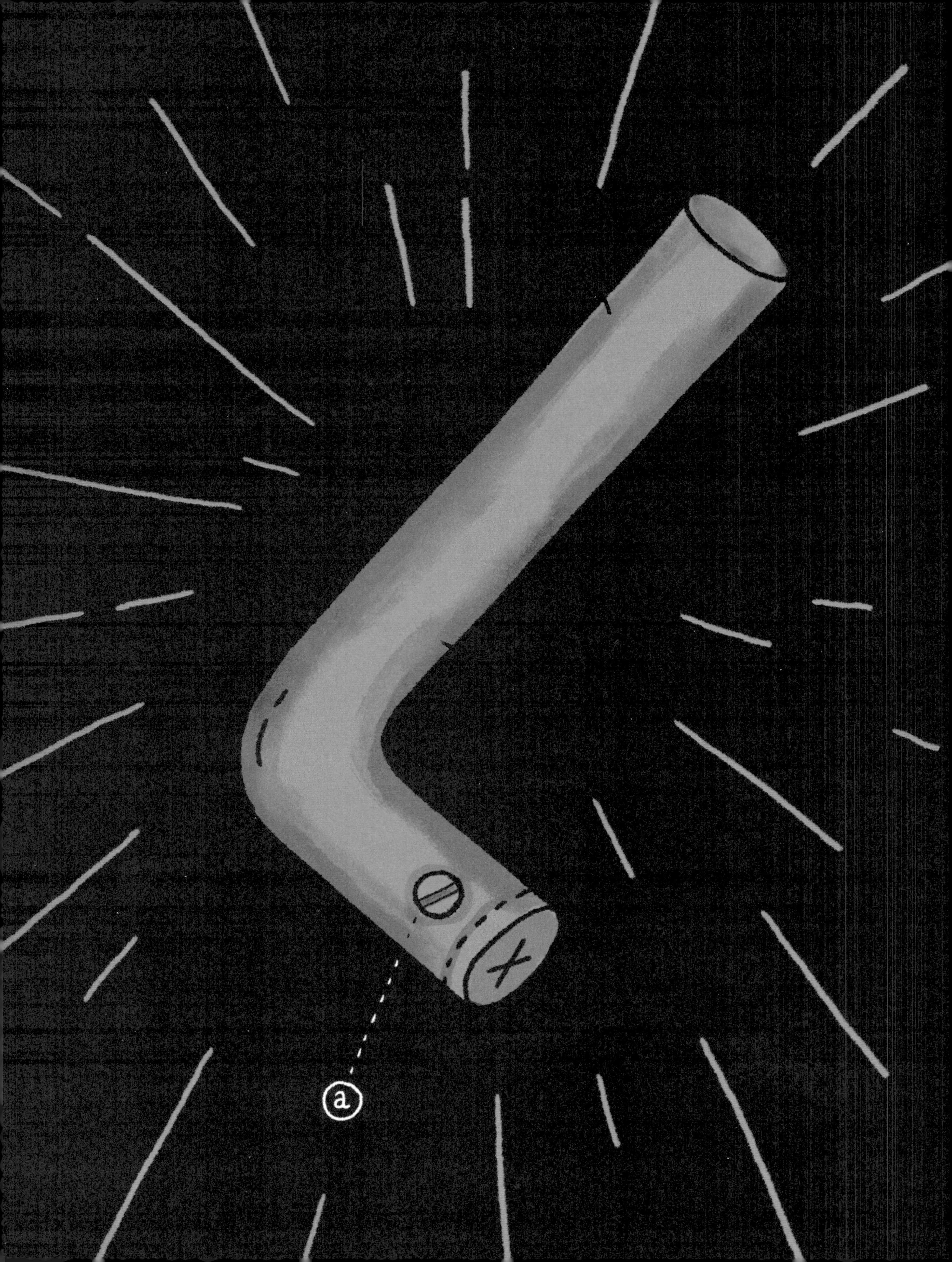
a

It was indeed. I cleared away what was left of the broken lever and prepared to fix the crank in its place. It fit like a glove. Wow! Littlehand really was way ahead of the game! Skim was cheering and waving his arms about like crazy. "We're in luck! We've got the right crank! Hooray!"

"What did I tell you? With a bit of luck, a tug on the right crank would set the world back in motion straight away," remarked Maurice in an unbearably smug voice. "to roll on rather like a ball made of ... you know what."

"For your information, Maurice," I said, "there's no greater luck in life than to have a really good friend. If Skim here hadn't turned up, we've never have got the Cog of Time restarted!"

Having pricked up his antennae, Maurice asked, "But are you sure that you really want aging back? Do you really want things to crumble, tear, fall apart, go moldy, stutter and stop working again? Do you want children to cry over broken toys? Do you want Professor Block to write a new history of aging?"

Skim and I looked at each other. We were of the same mind.

"OF COURSE WE DO!"

Skim grabbed one side of the crank, I grabbed the other, and we pulled ...

15: Ever

ages

comes

er

Since that time, everything again ages and falls apart as it should. I was so relieved when Skim, Maurice and I got the Cog of Time restarted! I can't know for sure, but I'd be very surprised if I ever get into a bigger a pickle than that one.

It's fair to say that the whole adventure made Skim and me pretty famous. My parents were terribly angry at first, of course. They made me write out the same sentence one thousand times:

NEREV ANAIG WLIL I SPOT THE COG OF TIEM!

Aagh! You've no idea what a chore it is to write typos when you have to concentrate on getting them right!

After that, though, everything was fine. Thanks to the help and resourcefulness of Steela the fifth-grader, Skim managed to get out of the chrono pressure suit. Dr Littlehand, by now the holder of an honorary Crystal Zilch for lifetime achievement, offered Skim a job as his personal assistant and tester of new inventions. Skim thanked him but turned down the offer. But guess what – I asked Littlehand if he'd take me on instead, and he did! Three times a week I go to the lab for new aging technologies, where I work on some really incredible stuff. I'll tell you all about it some other time.

Maurice went back to Uncle Remoudou and the dump, where he is happy pulling the peelings cart. When our paths cross, we wave to each other, but we never speak. Since the business we got into with the Cog of Time, the dung beetle has never said a single word, and I think that's for the best. By way of apology to Remoudou for stealing Maurice, I offered to work for him at the dump, but he waved my offer away. Now that our little adventure has made Maurice such a famous insect, he's prouder of him than ever, he says. He has entered Maurice for the dung run championships again, and they are in training for it.

Our stopping of the Great Cog of Time has gone down in history. First-graders at PSAT are taught about it as proof of the importance and benefits of aging. What do *you* think – is aging a good thing or not?

Anyway, now you know how much work it takes to make the things around you old, rusty and dilapidated. I'll bet there's such a thing within arm's reach of you at this very moment. Take a good look at it. There's something quite attractive about that muddy, worn shoe in the corner of the hall, isn't there? It may have once been new, clean and sweet-smelling, but it didn't stay like that for long before we came along and made it into a lovely old thing. That's what we're here for – at your service, from dawn till dusk, even during the night. So think of us sometimes, and wish us luck in our work! Bye for now!

Oh yes – a word of warning. The moment you read to the very end of this book, it will explode and burn to a crisp.

I'm joking, of course. But this is a joke that never gets old.

THE EDN

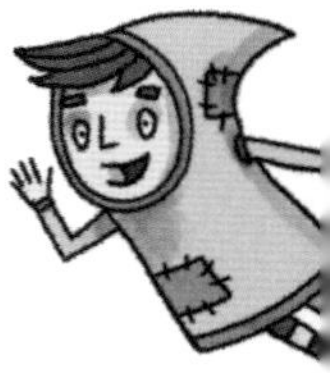

OL

TYPO

SKIM

MOM AND DAD TYPO

MOM AND DAD SKIM

UNCLE REMOUDOU

MAURICE

UNCLE BORE

BADEGG

WORMOLD

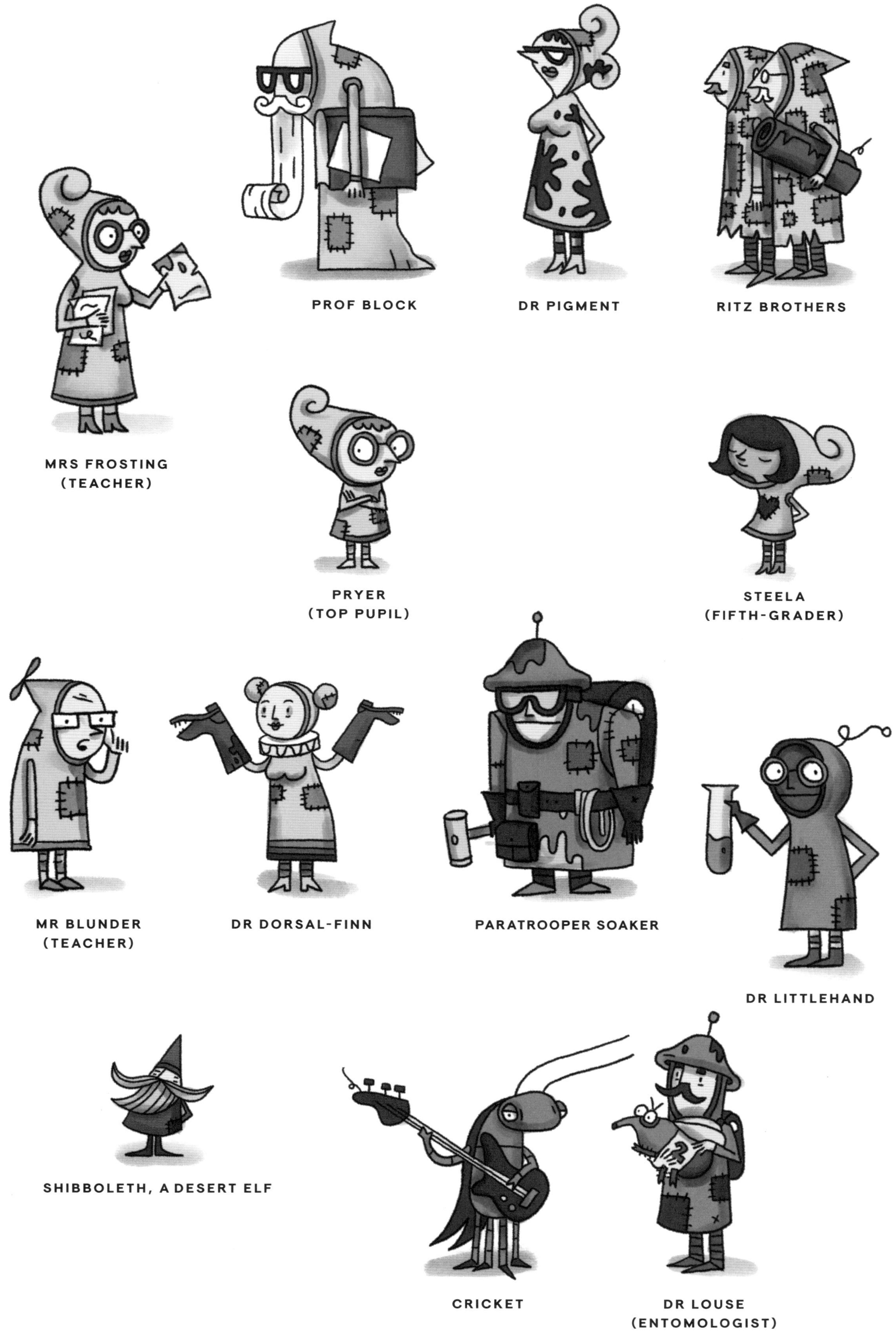
PROF BLOCK
DR PIGMENT
RITZ BROTHERS
MRS FROSTING
(TEACHER)
PRYER
(TOP PUPIL)
STEELA
(FIFTH-GRADER)
MR BLUNDER
(TEACHER)
DR DORSAL-FINN
PARATROOPER SOAKER
DR LITTLEHAND
SHIBBOLETH, A DESERT ELF
CRICKET
DR LOUSE
(ENTOMOLOGIST)

Typo and Skim

ILLUSTRATED
BY DANIEL ŠPAČEK

WRITTEN BY
TOMÁŠ KONČINSKÝ AND BARBORA KLÁROVÁ

GRAPHIC DESIGN AND TYPESETTING
(IN DOMAINE AND CLOWN)
BY PETR ŠTĚPÁN

COPY EDITING
BY VERONIKA KOPEČKOVÁ

EDITOR-IN-CHARGE:
PETR ELIÁŠ

FIRST U.S. EDITION 2022

PUBLISHED BY VAL DE GRÂCE BOOKS, NAPA, CALIFORNIA

AMERICAN TEXT © VAL DE GRÂCE BOOKS, 2016

ORIGINALLY PUBLISHED BY ALBATROS MEDIA A.S. IN PRAGUE IN 2016

© ALBATROS, 2016

© BARBORA KLÁROVÁ, 2016

© TOMÁŠ KONČINSKÝ, 2016

ILLUSTRATIONS © DANIEL ŠPAČEK, 2016

DESIGN © PETR ŠTĚPÁN, 2016

ART DIRECTION U.S. COVER: FABIOLA ZAMBON

ENTROPY DIAGRAM ON INSIDE COVER COURTESY OF SHUTTERSTOCK

ISBN 979-8-9858787-1-4

PRINTED BY ELEGANCE PRINTING (SHENZHEN) LTD.

ENGLISH TRANSLATION
BY ANDREW OAKLAND

U.S. EDITING
BY THOMAS HUMMEL

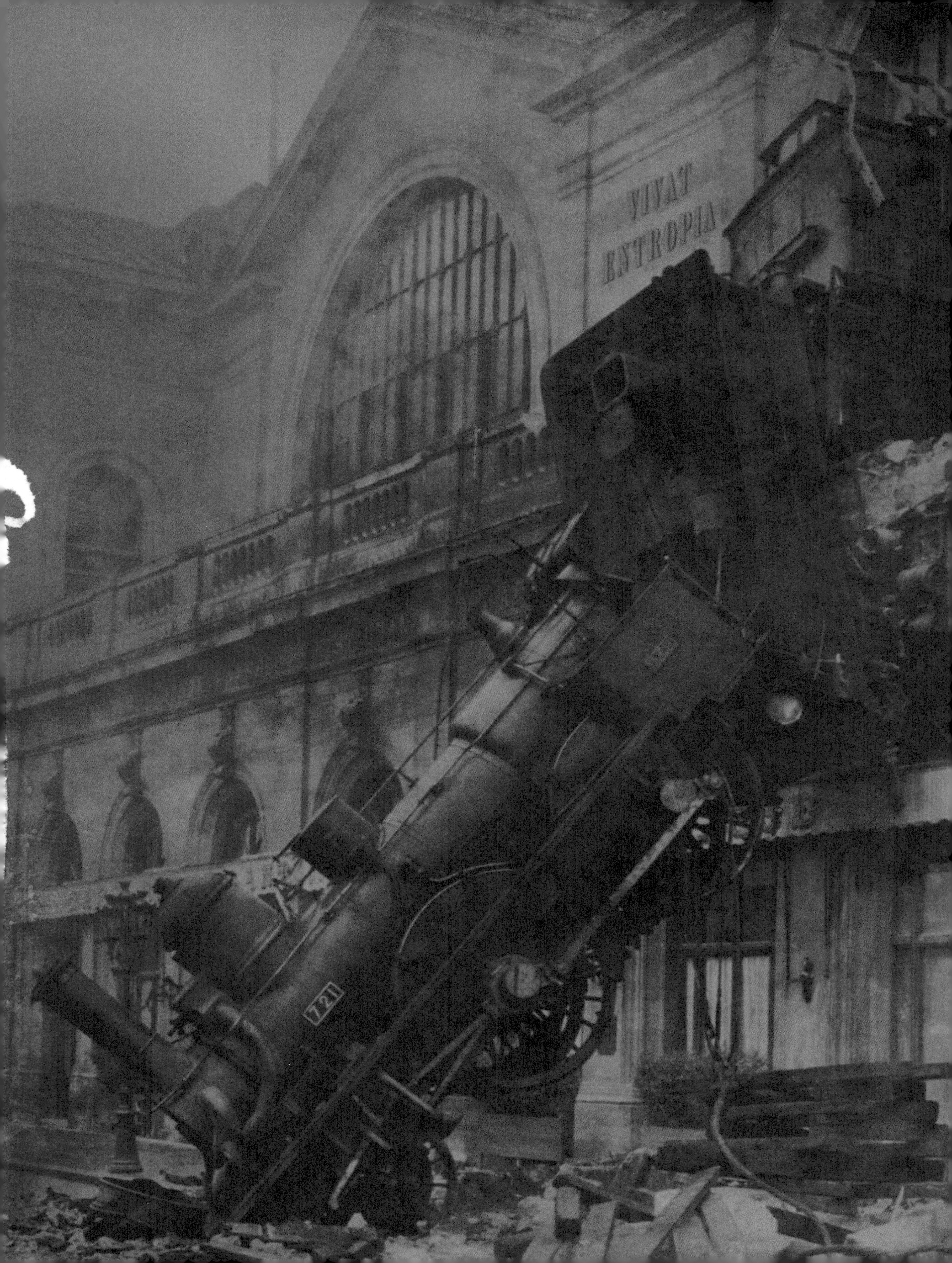
VIVAT
ENTROPIA
721

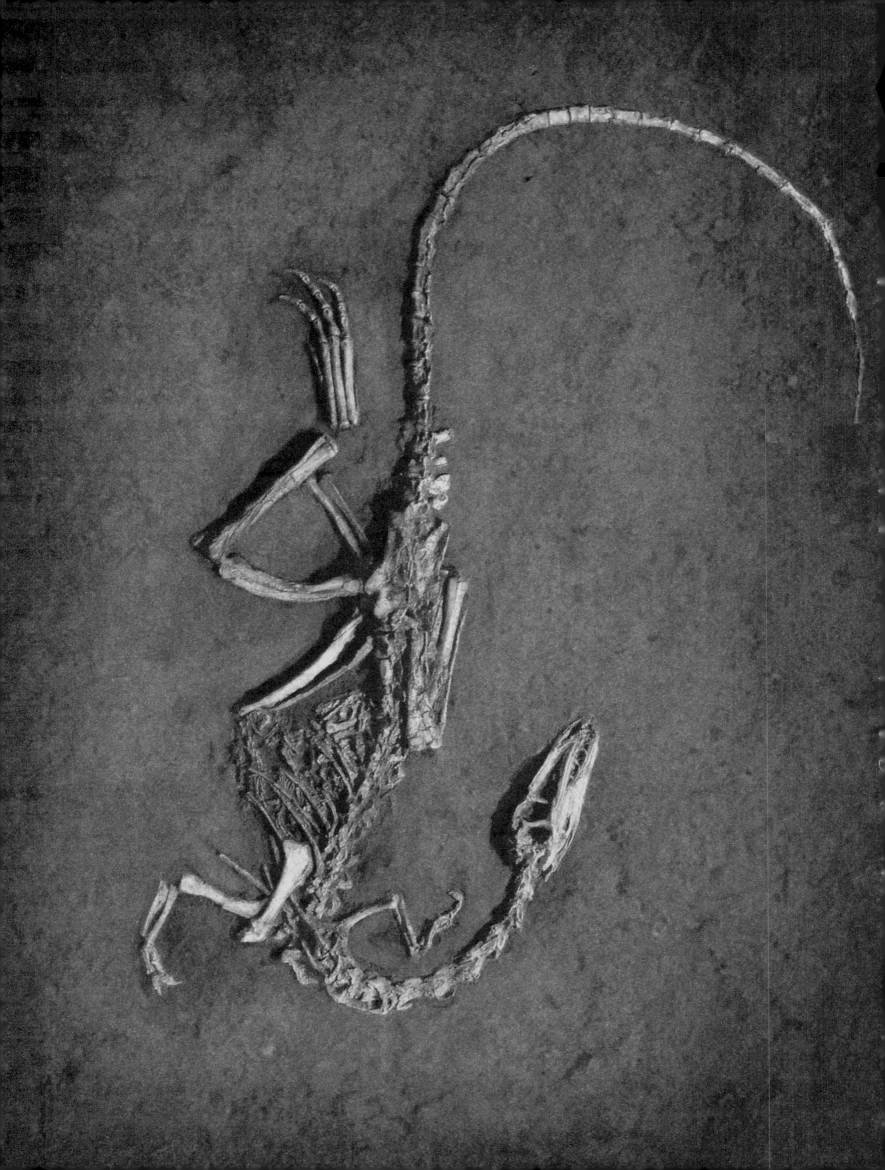